Take a Chance

USA TODAY BESTSELLING AUTHOR

Heather B. Moore

Take a Chance
A Prosperity Ranch Novel

Copyright © 2023 by Heather B. Moore
Paperback edition
All rights reserved

No part of this book may be reproduced in any form whatsoever without prior written permission of the publisher, except in the case of brief passages embodied in critical reviews and articles. This is a work of fiction. The characters, names, incidents, places, and dialogue are products of the author's imagination and are not to be construed as real.

Interior design by Cora Johnson
Edited by JL Editing Services and Lorie Humpherys
Cover design by Rachael Anderson
Cover image credit: Deposit Photos #409601732, SMEEitz
Published by Mirror Press, LLC
ISBN: 978-1-952611-35-3

PROSPERITY RANCH SERIES

One Summer Day
Steal My Heart
Not Over You
Seasoned With Love
Take a Chance

Chapter 1

Today should have been one of the happiest days of his life. But it was far from that.

His mom wasn't feeling well, so his dad had stayed back to take her to a doctor's appointment. His siblings all had major things going on in their lives—which was all understandable.

But...

It was Lane Prosper's graduation day from college. Even though it might be a bland major—business finance—Lane loved it. He and his oldest brother Holt had put together a business plan months ago in order to get their family ranch—Prosperity Ranch—squared up.

Just last night, Lane had gone over the accounting spreadsheets. He'd grinned for at least an hour because the past month had officially put the ranch into the black. Prosperity Ranch was profiting once again.

Yet...

"Lane Prosper!" the Dean of Student Admissions called into the microphone.

The cheer of the audience was measly at best. No one

really knew him. His main group of friends had been older, and had already graduated, and Lane had never replaced them. He'd taken as many credits as the Arizona university would allow in order to finish as soon as possible.

Lane pushed to his feet and strode to the stage. His black graduation gown flowed behind him since he hadn't bothered to zip it up, and his awkward-fitting graduation hat sat askew on his head. He'd rather be wearing his cowboy hat.

"Yay, Lane!" a woman screamed. A few people chuckled.

Without looking over, Lane knew the woman was Shelby. They'd gone on a date a few months ago, and well, she'd latched onto him like a bulldog smelling a fresh steak. Lane had become a professional Shelby-dodger. He knew exactly where to avoid her, and which times. But the graduation ceremony was the one thing he couldn't cut out on.

Lane kept his gaze forward, despite Shelby's next yell. "Smile for a picture!"

No, he wasn't posing for any picture. He walked up the stairs to the stage, keeping his gaze on those who were waiting to greet him.

Lane shook the hand of the woman holding out the diploma to him. Then he went on down the line, shaking administrators' hands, and then finally, Mrs. McEntire's, the Dean of the Business School.

"Congratulations, Mr. Prosper," Mrs. McEntire said, her exceptionally white teeth flashing.

He'd always wondered if she used teeth whitening on the daily.

"Thank you, ma'am."

Her smile dimpled. "Always so polite. Good luck with your family ranch."

The next name had been called, and the crowd burst out into applause. Whoever it was, they had family, and likely extended family, in town. It was too loud to explain to his professor that he wasn't going to be part of the ranch. No, that was all Holt. And rumor was that their second brother Knox would also jump in once his rodeo success tapered off. He was currently sitting at number one in the bull-riding world.

No pun intended...

Instead of heading back to his seat, and the potential of being cornered by Shelby, Lane left the auditorium. He had his diploma in hand, and he was done with this place. Besides, there was no family around to take pictures, so what was the use of staying?

"Lane?"

Great.

Shelby had seen him. And by the sound of it, she was following him pretty fast. It wasn't like he could start running. That would be much too impolite. But what would it take to get the message through to her?

He stopped and slowly turned, perspiration beading on his forehead.

Shelby was pretty—short, bouncy red hair, dancing blue eyes, and a quick smile. He hadn't even planned to ask her out, but she'd kept sitting by him at the library, trying to tell him about her life. So finally, he offered to chat over coffee at the campus café.

He might as well have proposed marriage by how excited she'd become. He couldn't back down then, so he went through with their... date?

After a full two hours at the café, and Shelby dumping her entire childhood on him, Lane had told her he wished her all the best. She'd offered her number, and he'd very politely declined, and she immediately burst into tears.

Lane should have walked away, but his conscience

wouldn't let him. They exchanged numbers, and the deluge of texts had begun.

At first, Lane answered a few, but then it soon became apparent that he was somehow leading her on by doing so. The next encounter, he'd told her that he wasn't interested in dating anyone. That he was graduating soon and leaving Arizona.

Shelby wasn't deterred in the least.

Nope. No way.

"Ohmygosh, Lane-y, you're one fast walker," Shelby gushed, all smiles.

Yep. She called him "Lane-y."

"Are you sure you aren't secretly on the track team? I mean, I think race-walking is an event? My cousin used to do those 5Ks, and I guess race-walking was an official event . . ."

The thing was, Shelby didn't leave much opportunity for Lane to respond. He literally had to interrupt. "I've got to head out, Shelby," he said. "Have a nice day."

"Wait, where are you going?" She'd scurried so close to him that she grasped his arm.

He sighed. There was no point in skirting the truth. "Packing. Heading out soon."

"You're leaving already? Where are you going? I can come visit. On the weekends, and when I have breaks. We could—"

"None of that is going to happen," Lane said. "I'm not going to be tied to anyone on campus. Starting fresh with everything. Hope you understand." He took a step back, then another.

Miraculously, she didn't follow. Her eyes blinked rapidly, and a tear fell down her cheek, then another. "This is goodbye? It can't be goodbye, Lane-y. I'll help you pack. I can bring over dinner and—"

"I'm fine," Lane said. "Thanks anyway." Then he turned and hurried off. Yeah, he might be race-walking after all.

Shelby called after him, but he didn't turn around. He crossed campus, taking a couple of detours in case she did decide to follow. Then he veered toward the music hall.

He'd never live it down if his brothers or sisters found out that he was a closet classical-music lover. They were all country, through and through. But he came here on days that he needed to decompress. Listening to the music students practicing relaxed him. Even when they messed up or had to repeat a section, he didn't mind.

Besides, he had some time on his hands. He didn't really want to hang around and watch all the students with their parents, or grab food at restaurants that would be filled with graduates. The university had served its purpose, except for one thing. He didn't have a job lined up yet. For weeks, he'd been sending out resumes to every financial institution he could think of between here and his home state of Texas, but the entry-level positions paid a pittance. And the higher-paid positions were looking for experience. So he'd expanded his search to states across the nation.

His phone rang just as he reached the music hall. For a second, he froze. What were the chances it was Shelby calling him?

It was a relief to see his oldest brother's name on the screen instead.

"Hey."

"Happy graduation," Holt's voice rumbled through the phone. "Sorry we couldn't make it."

"No worries." Lane paused on the sidewalk before he went inside. Hopefully, Shelby wouldn't spot him here. "I'm sure your wife wants you there for the delivery of your child."

Holt chuckled. "Well, yeah, if I want to stay married."

"Any news yet?"

"Just contractions that aren't progressing," Holt said. "They sent us home."

"What?" It wasn't like Lane knew a lot about delivering a baby—a human baby, at least. Horses, that he knew. But if his sister-in-law was in labor . . .

"Yeah." Holt sighed. "We're just hanging at home. Oh wait—uh, gotta go, bro."

"What's going on—" Lane started, but his brother had already hung up. He exhaled, thinking about Macie and Holt, and hoped all would go well with the birth of their baby. Their relationship had been a rocky road, and Lane was happy they were through the rocky stuff, and increasing their family now.

With a quick glance around to assure himself there was no Shelby in sight, Lane pushed through the double glass doors. In the reflection of the glass, he saw the ridiculous-looking graduation gown—out of place now. He tugged it off along with his graduation cap. He'd sent his mom a selfie just before the ceremony, and that would have to do.

As Lane continued into the main auditorium, he heard music—piano music. Good, someone was playing one of those classical pieces. Lane wouldn't be able to identify the composer to save his life, but he'd heard this piece before.

He checked the time on his cell phone. His mom was at her doctor's appointment by now. Mom was a breast-cancer survivor, so any illness, no matter how mild, was taken seriously. And now with Macie potentially having her baby soon—there was just a lot going on back home in Prosper.

Lane would celebrate the next time he saw his family. For now, he'd just sit in the dark and listen to someone's piano rehearsal. Let Shelby get tired of chasing him down. Maybe someone else would catch her eye. He could only hope. If not, he'd be out of here tomorrow anyway.

He headed through the auditorium door, stepping into the dark. At the end of the long center aisle, the stage was highlighted by a single spotlight on a lustrous grand piano.

A woman with long, wavy, dark hair sat at the piano, her posture erect, her eyes closed, her fingers dancing over the keys as she played.

He should have known it was *her*... Because the song was familiar, and he'd listened to her play it before.

Lane scanned for the guy—the one who was always with her, usually scrolling through his phone and not paying attention. Probably her boyfriend.

But the guy wasn't in any of the front rows. Lane surveyed the rest of the dark auditorium. Huh. No one else was in here. As usual, Lane took one of the back rows, leaned back in the velvet-cushioned chair, and propped up his cowboy boots on the seat in front of him.

No one could see him doing so—besides, they were his dressy ones. Polished deep enough that he could probably see his reflection in them.

It took only a handful of minutes for Lane to get caught up in the piano music. This woman was talented enough to be professional was his guess. Weren't there more prestigious music programs than a random university in Arizona? Not that Lane was the best judge, or the expert on classical piano players, but whoever the dark-haired woman was, she was the best he'd ever heard. Including those he'd pulled up on YouTube.

Lane put his phone on silent so texts would only vibrate, then he rested his head against the back of his seat and closed his eyes. The music swelled and dipped, then swelled again, taking Lane's heart right along with it.

Maybe he was just missing his family, or maybe tomorrow's move back home was messing with his emotions.

But his throat had tightened right along with the melancholy of the notes coming from the front of the auditorium.

Lane didn't know how long he'd been listening, or if he'd in fact dozed off, but the next thing he knew, the music had come to an abrupt halt.

He opened his eyes, and after a couple of seconds, they adjusted to the light up on the stage. The woman was standing, her arms folded, as she faced her . . . boyfriend?

His voice was a low rumble, and Lane couldn't quite make out the words. But it was clear they were arguing. Lane tensed. What were they discussing? The woman wasn't speaking at all, nor was she moving.

The boyfriend was certainly animated, but his voice didn't get loud enough to hear his words.

Lane slowly lowered his boots so as to not make a sound. He rose to his feet and walked quietly to the end of the row.

The boyfriend threw up his hands, a scowl on his face. The woman took a step back, shaking her head, her lips pursed. Arms still crossed.

The boyfriend moved toward her, and she stepped back again.

Lane's pulse was racing like a Texas thunderstorm for some reason. Every muscle in his body had coiled.

Then, suddenly, the boyfriend pivoted and headed across the stage. Muttering. Probably cursing. The guy disappeared behind a heavy black drape, then a door shut. He was gone.

The tension seemed to leave with him.

Interesting.

Lane's gaze cut to the woman again. She didn't seem overly upset. She simply sat down on the piano bench and began to play again. This song wasn't the melancholy one of before; this song was faster paced. Full of passion? Anger? Both?

Take a Chance

He was mesmerized as he watched her slice through the music, her hands flying against the keys. She was talented, sure—beyond this college—but *this*... Her playing right now was brilliant and powerful and beautiful.

Lane couldn't even sit down. He couldn't relax. No, he stayed on his feet, and when the music reached its thundering conclusion, he clapped.

It took him a second to realize what he'd done. Not only had he given himself away, but he'd likely scared her.

She leapt to her feet and shielded her eyes against the spotlight. "Brady? Why are you still here?"

Lane cleared his throat because there was still some emotion lodged there. "I'm not Brady."

The woman walked to the edge of the stage, and Lane tried to come up with something to say. "Sorry to have disturbed your practice, ma'am," he said. "I was . . . I was taking a breather and heard you playing. I didn't mean to . . . well, your talent is beyond description, and I couldn't help but clap when you finished . . ."

His voice trailed off when he realized she was standing at the edge of the stage, her hands on her hips, her eyes narrowed as she searched him out.

Lane walked a few steps down the aisle, then halted. "I'll go now. Sorry to disturb." He turned and headed toward the main doors. He didn't want to go. He wanted to stay. Listen to her practice. But even more, he wanted to ask her what had happened between her and "Brady." Why Lane cared, he didn't know.

Tomorrow, he was leaving Arizona, and he'd never see this woman again. There was no reason to ask if he could stay and listen.

"Wait," she said, her tone so soft he almost didn't hear it.

Lane turned around. To his surprise, the woman was walking up the aisle toward him.

Chapter 2

AVA SAMPSON HAD NO IDEA why she'd told this man to wait. She was alone in a dark auditorium with a stranger, who was apparently listening to her practice. How she felt about that, she wasn't sure, but right now, she wanted to know who he was. If he was a creeper. If she should call security. If he was one of Brady's friends—spying on her.

This man was tall, broad-shouldered. Blond. And as she got closer, she saw that his blue eyes cut through all the dimness of the room. He was also wearing well-worn jeans, a button-down shirt that appeared as if it had never seen an iron, and cowboy boots. He wasn't really the type of friend Brady would have, so she dismissed any connection to him.

But what was this cowboy doing *here*? Listening to her piano concertos?

There were a couple of country-music bands on campus—maybe he played guitar for one of them?

She stopped in the aisle because she was plenty close now. Close enough to know he wasn't wearing expensive cologne like Brady did. This man smelled like the spring day outside. And he was staring at her like he couldn't believe she'd approached him.

Take a Chance

Ava folded her arms. "Are you a student? Staff?" She doubted staff, but she was still asking. "Are you in the wrong building? The agriculture department is on the other side of campus."

The man grimaced as he rubbed the back of his neck. "Nah."

Heat flooded Ava's face. She was being rude. But she'd been surprised by his clapping. Startled. "I'm sorry, I didn't mean—" Wait, why was *she* apologizing? And why had she stopped this man? "I guess you like piano music?"

He dropped his hand, then shoved both of them into the front pockets of his jeans. "I don't rightly know, ma'am. I like *your* piano music."

She stared at him. "Have you listened to me before?"

He nodded. "A few times. And other musicians. Whoever is practicing when I'm taking a break."

She tilted her head. She should leave this man alone, let him go. Get back to practicing. "I don't mean to be rude, but I don't really take you for being a classical-music junkie."

One side of his mouth lifted. "I don't mind the straight talk, ma'am. If you'd have asked me a few months ago if I'd ever listened to anything classical, the answer would have been in the negative."

Ava blinked. He didn't speak like a hick. Oh, he had a southern drawl, but his language wasn't small town. "You don't have to call me *ma'am*. I'm guessing I'm younger than you?"

His gaze moved from her eyes and swept downward. Was he checking her out?

"Point taken, miss," he said.

Now heat flushed her cheeks for a different reason. His gaze was so . . . direct and steady.

"You know, there's a concert here tomorrow night," Ava

said. Why was she still talking? "Solo pieces. A competition, actually. You might enjoy it."

"Are you competing?"

His question was unexpected, but it shouldn't have been. "Yes. I'm playing."

"Which piece? The one you just played?"

"No . . . that one isn't ready for the public." She paused. "I make a lot of mistakes still."

His gaze didn't move from her face. "If you play it, rough edges and all, you'll win the competition, miss."

"Oh?" She wanted to laugh, but she was flattered, too. What could this cowboy really know about her competition or how important it was for her to win? "I don't want to be rude, but—"

"But what does a guy like me know about music like yours?" he finished for her.

She gave a soft laugh, a nervous laugh. "Exactly."

He dipped his head. "I don't know any of the technical terms. Heck, I don't even know the names of the pieces you play, but I've heard a lot of practicing over the months. None of them play like you just played."

The breath left Ava for a moment. The compliment was heartfelt and probably the most sincere she'd ever received. "Well . . . I hope the judges appreciate my music as much as you do, sir."

"Lane."

She raised her brows.

"I'm not a *sir*, that's my father," he said. "Name's Lane Prosper."

"My name is Ava." She didn't give her last name because, well, that would have been too much information.

"Nice to meet you, Ava," he said. "Best of luck tomorrow night. I wish I could watch, but I'm headed out first thing in the morning."

"Oh, all right." She was curious. Too curious. She should quit asking questions, so she didn't stop him again when he turned and headed out of the auditorium.

After he left, the place felt vast and empty. Missing something. Which was silly.

Nothing was missing. Everything was in its place. Or would be when she won the competition tomorrow night and earned herself scholarship money, which would pay for her next year of tuition, something she couldn't miss out on.

The competition would be a sweet consolation, because this week had been the pits. A few days ago, she'd discovered Brady was dating other women behind her back. The strange thing was that Ava wasn't furious at him. She was more disappointed that she wouldn't be joining him on the summer tour they'd planned together. Now she had to figure out another way to earn money for tuition that paid more than minimum wage. Thus, the music competition.

She turned to head toward the stage, but she noticed something hanging on the back of a chair. A jacket? She picked up what looked like a graduation gown. A cap tumbled to the ground.

She knew it was graduation today, which was the perfect opportunity for her to practice in the empty auditorium. But if this belonged to Lane Prosper—had he just graduated? She snatched both the gown and cap, then headed through the auditorium doors.

But there was a wall beyond the doors. Or a man-wall that she'd run straight into.

"Oh," she gasped.

"Sorry." The man grasped her arms to steady her.

Ava looked up. Sure enough, it was *him*.

"You forgot your stuff," she said.

At the same time, he said, "I forgot my stuff."

Ava laughed.

Lane smiled.

Her insides sighed. Wait. That wasn't supposed to happen. She'd literally broken up with her boyfriend a few days ago, and she was determined to go solo for a while. A long while.

Was there really harm, though, in appreciating a good-looking man—cowboy? He had to be a student. He'd never said, but she was good at putting two and two together.

She handed the graduation gown and cap to him, and their fingers brushed. His were warm despite the air conditioning of the auditorium.

"Thanks, miss."

"Ava."

His smile grew. "Ava. Thank you again." Then he turned to leave.

"Wait," Ava blurted out. "You—did you graduate today?"

He turned around. The lights outside the auditorium had revealed that his blue eyes were quite remarkable, the blue of a cloudless sky. "I did."

"In agriculture?" she teased.

Another smile stole onto his face. "Not exactly. Business finance."

She couldn't help the surprise that apparently crossed her face, because he added, "Not all cowboys are hicks, you know."

Dang. Her cheeks heated. Could he see her blush? "Agriculture is a perfectly respectable major, *if* you were to major in that, but since you didn't . . ."

"Since I didn't . . . ?" he prompted.

"Oh, never mind." She puffed out a breath. "Congratulations on your graduation. I hope it all goes well for you—in the finance world, or banking. Or whatever it is you're doing

Take a Chance

after this. I guess you're on to bigger and better things now?" She was totally rambling. How was his gaze so steady and penetrating at the same time?

"Not exactly," Lane said. "Or at least not yet."

"Are you interviewing for jobs or something?"

"Trying to," Lane said. "I've got no real-world work experience. I plowed through school without pausing for an internship, so I'm hitting a wall to get past the entry-level stuff."

Ava nodded. "Yeah, a catch-22."

He leaned against the nearby pillar and folded his arms, his gaze assessing her. "Exactly."

"I'm sure you'll find something soon," she said, trying not to stare at the way his position displayed the ropey muscles of his forearms. It was clear that this college student wasn't sitting at a desk at all hours. "I mean, finances are pretty straightforward. Not like the music industry, where everything's subjective."

His brows drew together, and she found it kind of adorable that he was listening to her so intently.

"You can't really think your music is subjective," he said. "I mean, even a cowboy like me was mesmerized."

Her pulse did a little leap. "You were mesmerized?"

"I was."

He said it so matter-of-factly that she didn't think he was trying to flirt or anything. Was he? "Well, thank you. I just hope the judges agree with you tomorrow night, or I might be the next waitress at the campus café."

"You lost me there, Ava."

More sighing on the inside at the way he pronounced her name. "It's just... well, I'm not on any academic scholarship, and the music scholarships are hard to get. So... I'm hoping to win tomorrow and use the money for next year's tuition."

"I think you have a good chance," he said in another

15

matter-of-fact tone. "You know which piece I think you should play."

She grimaced. "Yeah . . ."

"I double-dog dare you."

Ava laughed. "No one *dares* each other anymore. Not unless you're like a ten-year-old boy."

Lane shrugged. "I've been called worse."

This only made Ava more curious. Why was she so intrigued by this finance-major cowboy? She needed to tell the fluttering in her stomach to calm down. "Well, to accept a dare, I'd have to get some sort of prize if I win."

Lane's brows shot up. "If you win, don't you get the prize money?"

"Yeah, right." Beyond the main hall, Ava could see families of graduates walking through campus. Some had stopped by the statue of the university founder to take pictures. "Oh, are you missing pictures with your family?"

Lane's eyes flashed with something she couldn't describe.

"They all had other obligations," he said.

Ava blinked. She had a small family—just her and her mom—but her mom would never miss a big event. "Too far to travel?" she prompted, because she was wondering where he was from . . .

"Most of them are in Texas, if that's what you're asking."

She was the one who shrugged this time. "I could have probably guessed Texas. Or maybe Oklahoma."

"*Ouch.* Please don't mix me up with anyone from Oklahoma."

She laughed. "I'm sure they're great people, too."

"I'm sure they are." He smirked. "I almost got disowned for coming to college in Arizona, but they were the ones with the scholarship offer."

"Scholarship, huh? So you're a smarty pants?"

Lane chuckled.

His laugh was nice and low. The sighing inside of her returned.

"No one says *smarty pants* anymore. Unless you're a ten-year-old girl."

"Touché, Lane Prosper."

His smile was warm, open, and made her feel like the sun had just come out after a cloudy day.

He straightened from his pillar. "I should get going. Gotta get some packing done. Big move tomorrow."

She nodded, feeling an emptiness move through her—why? "Well, good luck with all of that. If you get delayed or anything, I'll be performing tomorrow night." *Oh, sheesh.* Was she feeding him a pickup line? "I mean . . . You have a good life."

Her face was likely flaming now, and she had to really stop herself from rambling. Back to practice. She turned and headed toward the auditorium doors.

"Wait."

Chapter 3

LANE SHOULD LET AVA GET back to her practice, but he'd seen the interest in her eyes when she looked at him. And, well, he was interested, too. Especially since it seemed that she'd ditched her boyfriend. What had happened there anyway? It wasn't really his business... yet.

Ava turned around. Her brown eyes reminded him of the color of the cinnamon his mom stirred into hot cocoa at Christmastime. There weren't really any other times hot cocoa made sense in Texas.

Lane knew he was being bold in asking, especially since he was heading out of Arizona tomorrow. And he'd basically used that excuse on Shelby. Yet, Ava was no Shelby...

The words had left his mouth before he could force them back. "Do you want to grab a drink, or maybe something to eat? If you're hungry, that is. I mean, after your practice, of course. I can wait."

He sounded like he was trying to pick her up. Or he was desperate enough to hang around until she was finished practicing. That wasn't it, though...

She didn't say anything for a few seconds, and Lane

suddenly wondered if she was secretly laughing at him. "I mean, unless you have someone who might object?" he hedged.

Her eyes glinted, and a small smile lifted the edge of her lips. "Or if *I* object?"

"That, too."

She folded her arms, reminding him of when she'd been facing down her ex-boyfriend, except she didn't look displeased right now. In fact, she looked . . . pleased.

"I have to finish my practice."

Lane's pulse skyrocketed. She wasn't turning him down. "I can wait."

"I thought you said you had to pack?" she suggested.

"I did say that, and it's true, though I'd rather listen to you play." He was quite enjoying the flush to her cheeks, but that wasn't why he'd complimented her. It was simply the truth, and there was no reason to skirt around it.

"Suit yourself." She turned again and tugged the door open.

Lane tossed his cap and gown into the nearby trash, then grabbed the door over her head and held it open. "You never answered me," he said, following her inside.

"About what?" The only light came from the stage, and she was nearly swallowed up by the darkness.

"About whether someone else might object."

"Oh, that." She stopped, and Lane stopped just before running into her. "Brady is history."

"Did you date for a while?"

"A few months, but . . . he's apparently quite the ladies' man."

She was looking at him. Peering at him, in fact. As if to ask if he was one, too.

Lane lifted his hands. "His loss."

Ava smirked, then turned and walked toward the stage.

Lane followed. There was no reason for him to sit in the back anymore. Besides, he liked her smirk. And a few other things about her. Following her like this, he caught her scent—something citrusy. Lemon? Orange?

She turned her head, and he hoped she hadn't caught him checking her out. "Do you play?"

"The piano? Uh, not really. Unless you count 'Mary Had a Little Lamb.'"

She slowed her step. "Oh, that's at least something. You read music?"

"Yes, ma'am."

She had dimples when she smiled, and he had the urge to touch her cheeks, but he kept his hands in his pockets.

They'd reached the stage, and she stopped and looked up at him. "So if you read music, you must play something. Let me guess, guitar?"

He looked up at the ceiling, then released his breath. When he looked at her again, he admitted, "I do play guitar. I'm not bad, but I'm not that good, either. Am I a cliché now?"

She only smiled. "I guess we'll find out."

"How so?"

She didn't answer his question. "Have a seat, Lane Prosper. And keep your applause to yourself."

He chuckled as she climbed the stairs. He sat in the front row. It might be a bit close for some people, but not for him.

She found her way to the piano and settled on the bench. Instead of playing one of the pieces he'd heard before, she ran through a group of scales. Up and down the keyboard, switching keys each time. Rising and falling. Faster, then slower. Even her scales were mesmerizing.

Lane leaned forward, watching everything about her. Memorizing details. It would be a long drive back to Prosper,

Texas, and this would give him something to think about. The gentle sway of her wavy hair. The arch of her neck. The flutter of her lashes as she closed her eyes and began a slow melody. The way her fingers seemed to float above the piano keys. The dip of her shoulder as she played something in a lower octave.

Ava was stunning. Both in talent and in appearance. He was probably a fool for sitting here for another hour and wanting to spend more time with her. Was it possible to have a heart broken even before falling for someone?

He scoffed at himself.

Apparently it was loud enough for Ava to hear, because she stopped playing and looked over her shoulder. "Something wrong?"

"Uh, no, nothing's wrong." Lane exhaled. "I was just in my head, I guess."

She lifted a dark brow. "Oh, and what's on your mind?"

He leaned back in his seat and propped one boot atop his knee. "Ignore me. Pretend that you have an audience of hundreds. There might be some distractions. You should play your competition piece. You know, get that one polished up."

She stared at him for a few seconds, then blinked. "You're kind of bossy, you know that? I mean, for a guy who doesn't know much about classical music and has probably never been to a concert full of it."

"You're right, but maybe that makes my opinion the most authentic."

Her laughter was as beautiful as her music. When she stopped laughing, he was grinning; he couldn't help it. He'd had his phone on silent since first coming to the auditorium, but now the screen lit up with his mom calling.

He stared at the incoming call, panic darting through him.

"You can answer it," Ava said.

"Hello?" Lane wondered if it was good or bad that his mom was calling—or would it be his dad if the news was bad?

"Happy graduation, honey," his mom said, her voice lovely and familiar over the phone.

"Thanks, Mom." Lane willed his pulse to stop jumping. "How did the doctor's appointment go?"

"Oh, fine. I'm fine. How was the ceremony? Were there a lot of people there?"

Lane frowned. "You're *fine*? As in, *completely* fine? What did the doctor say, exactly?"

His mom's laugh was soft. "He said that I have a cold. Imagine that. The men in my life overreacted—more specifically, your father. We should have just gone to Arizona. The doctor's appointment could have waited."

Lane wasn't sure if he should laugh or just sigh with relief. He didn't care that his mom hadn't come to his graduation—he was just glad she wasn't giving him bad news. "You did the right thing, Mom," he said. "I'd rather know you're all right than force you to sit through a bunch of long talks about the same thing—our bright futures."

He pictured his mom's smile over the phone. "You're a sweetheart, Lane. Thanks for always just being you."

Lane's mind was racing, though. "Any news on Macie's baby?"

"Not yet," his mom said. "They're at the hospital, but it could be hours yet. Now, Dad wants to talk to you, too."

Lane glanced at Ava. She didn't act perturbed at all. Should he head out of the auditorium, though? He was cutting into her practicing time.

His dad's voice boomed into the phone before Lane could decide. Rex Prosper was no quiet or timid man, but he certainly was ruled over by his wife. As mayor of Prosper and owner of Prosperity Ranch, Dad was a self-made man with a lot of respect in their community.

"How does it feel to have a college degree under your belt?" his dad asked.

Lane had no doubt Ava could hear every word, because her smile appeared.

He felt like smiling, too. "It feels great. No more homework. No more classes. No more doing case studies for free."

His dad chuckled. "You know the offer still stands, and Holt agrees with me. You can run the finances for the ranch and pick up more clients in Prosper. Farmers make poor accountants."

Lane nodded. "I know, Dad. Thanks. I just . . . I don't really want to be an accountant." He pictured his dad frowning. No matter how many times Lane explained to his dad about his major, his dad always reduced it to crunching numbers like a CPA.

"Any job leads?"

Lane released a breath. Ava was still listening and watching, seeming quite content to be his sole audience.

"Nothing since we talked this morning."

"Well, you know, Bill over at—"

"Look, Dad, I'm actually with a . . . friend. I should go—"

"Friend? A woman? Did you finally start dating—"

"Bye, Dad." Lane hung up the phone and slipped it into his pocket. "Sorry about that."

Ava's smile appeared. "I found it interesting. So your mom had a doctor's appointment, but she's fine, your sister or sister-in-law is in labor, and you aren't dating anyone?"

Lane's nodded. "That's the simple version."

"What's the real version?"

Did she really want to know? "My mom is a cancer survivor, so we all overreact a bit when she gets sick. My sister-in-law Macie is married to my oldest brother, but she used to be married to my second-oldest brother. And no . . . I'm not dating anyone. It seems that I'm the single-date guy on campus. Never quite get to that second date."

Ava's brows rose. "Oh, that's a story I want to hear."

The back auditorium doors opened, and a couple of guys walked in carrying violin cases.

Ava peered at the new people. "Time's up, I guess."

Lane rose to his feet. "Sorry for the phone call. I didn't know—"

"It's fine. Besides, I'm starving, and I think you asked me out. First date, and all."

Chapter 4

Why was she flirting with Lane Prosper?

Ava should really mellow out, because the guy was leaving tomorrow, and she still hadn't processed what had happened with Brady. Not fully. Spotting him a few days ago at the campus café with Natalie had definitely triggered Ava. Her dad had been unfaithful to her mom. And no matter how much Brady tried to explain it away, the knot in Ava's chest told her she'd lost all trust in him.

And it hadn't been the first time. She'd seen him at the library with different girls, studying one on one. She'd confronted him once, and he'd said it was just for their class together. But the looks, the small touches, the smiles . . . those were all real. Ava hadn't imagined them.

And now, here she was flirting with a guy she'd just met, who'd be heading out in a handful of hours. Maybe her mind was in turmoil or something, and the pain would come later. The hurt. The disappointment.

Why wasn't she in her apartment crying over Brady? All week, she'd gone about her normal routine, not even sad over him. And now, she was walking alongside this guy from Texas whose gaze was steady and who spoke direct words.

Lane opened the auditorium door for her, and she stepped into the main lobby. The light took a few seconds to adjust to. They headed out of the building, Lane holding open the door again. It was a small thing, but something Ava appreciated. Brady was... Well, everything was fifty-fifty with him. They paid for their own meals, which Ava was fine with, since they were both students. Although Brady was rather wealthy, and Ava was dead broke. It hadn't mattered. Not really. That was what Ava had told herself over and over when Brady would pick her up in his sports car wearing something new again, then make sure they split the tip at a nice restaurant—usually a place he'd picked. Ava was just fine with a turkey sandwich at a café.

She pushed those thoughts away as she walked across campus with Lane Prosper. Their easy chatter from the auditorium had seemed to fade, but the silence wasn't awkward. Surprisingly.

The late afternoon was sunny and warm, but the wind had kicked up. Whatever cold from the air-conditioned auditorium that had been soaking into her skin during her piano playing now seeped out.

"Any preferences?" Lane asked.

She'd been so caught up in her thoughts that she almost startled. "Oh, uh, the campus café is fine."

It was a place she'd stopped suggesting to Brady because he'd said the food was terrible. But it was close, quick, and Ava didn't mind convenience.

"Sounds good," Lane said. "They have a mean BLT."

"Oh, I like that, too," Ava said, looking over at him. His blue eyes were on her again. The wind had stirred his hair into messy waves.

"Wheat or white bread?" he asked.

Ava laughed. "Wheat. And you?"

"White."

They both smiled at each other, and Ava's pulse skittered. His smile was so easy-going, natural, and open. She'd never felt such instant attraction to someone. It must be some weird rebound thing, she decided. Her heart was completely confused. Probably in pain over Brady, though she hadn't allowed herself to feel it yet.

As they approached the campus café, it was clear the wait would be long. The line wrapped around the inside of the café, then out the door.

"Plan B?" Lane said.

Ava smoothed her hair back from her face. The wind was stronger now, and some clouds had started to gather. "Are we walking or do you have a car?"

His gaze cut to hers. She'd probably surprised him.

"My truck's parked in the next lot over."

"Of course you have a *truck*."

His brows lifted. "And . . ."

"And nothing."

He didn't look convinced. "Ever been in a truck?" he teased.

"Of course," she sputtered. "I mean, it's been a while. My dad had one, but he took off when I was a kid. Abandoned my mom and me to create a new family with another woman."

Lane looked as if he'd been punched in the gut. She hadn't meant to be so cavalier, but she'd recited it so many times that the words had tumbled out.

"Sorry, Ava, I didn't mean to bring up something hurtful."

She pushed more hair behind her ears, but the wind tugged it free again. "It's been a long time, but thank you. I should have probably stopped at *yes*. Didn't need to spill my backstory so fast."

"You can tell me whatever you want." He combed a hand through his hair as the wind increased.

A couple of students ran past them toward the café, holding onto their caps so they wouldn't blow away in the wind.

"Thanks," she said. A gust of wind rattled a nearby trashcan. It toppled and fell.

Lane righted the garbage can, but it was too late to save the trash—it was already blowing its way across campus.

He moved closer to Ava. "Hey, looks like we might be getting a dust storm." He pointed to the east, where the dark clouds were in fact not clouds of rain, but dust.

Another gust whipped the nearby trees, making them rattle and sway.

"Come on, let's get to my truck, unless you have a better idea." Lane had to speak louder over the sound of the wind.

"Your truck's fine," Ava called back.

"This way." He started walking, and Ava followed.

The wind tugged at her clothing and seemed to steal her breath. She closed her eyes partway against the flying dust and particles in the air.

"We should run for it," Lane's voice rumbled next to her. "It's coming in quick."

She squinted toward the dust clouds. They were so much closer now.

Lane grasped her hand, and she held on as they ran toward the parking lot. Other people were hurrying across campus, trying to find shelter.

Lane kept ahold of her hand as he led her to a red truck that had seen better days—maybe twenty years ago. He unlocked the door and opened it for her, and she hopped in.

Instantly, the wind and dust stopped pelting her. She blinked the dust out of her eyes as Lane hurried around the front of the truck and climbed in the driver's side.

"Wow," he said after slamming his door shut. "That's sure moving fast." He looked over at her. "Want some water? I think I have a mouth full of dirt."

"Sure." She looked about the cab and saw only one water bottle in a cup holder. "But if that's yours, I can wait."

"It's new," he said, handing it over. "Take the curse off of it."

When she hesitated, he said, "I have four siblings. It's not a big deal."

So she took the first swig, then handed over the water. She was feeling better. Less gritty.

Lane drank half the water bottle, then put it back into the cup holder. He leaned toward her and reached down. Then he snatched a cowboy hat that had been at her feet.

"Oh, I'm sorry, I don't think I stepped on it."

"It's fine. Been through a lot, so a couple of footprints wouldn't matter if you had stepped on it."

She watched as he set the hat on his head. His profile with that hat was sure . . . nice. Something twinged in her stomach.

He started the truck, and it roared to life.

Why did so many trucks sound the same? She couldn't help but think of her dad, and it made her blink harder.

Instead of pulling out of the parking lot, Lane adjusted the AC knob. "Hopefully today is a good day. The AC doesn't always work."

Cool air was filling the cab, though, so today must be a good day. "Can't you get it fixed? I mean Arizona isn't really the state to have your AC break down."

"Tried, more than once, but she's finicky."

"*She*?"

"Yep."

Ava smiled. "You seem quite attached to this truck. You had it long?"

"Used to be my dad's. My two older brothers have newer trucks, but I like this one." His gaze shifted from her to outside the windows. "Wow, this is some dust storm."

Ava followed his gaze. She'd been in several dust storms, and this one was no different. It was like a brown fog—hard to see past more than a few cars in the parking lot. At least it seemed like everyone had found shelter. The wind rocked the truck and would have been eerie if she'd been by herself. But sitting here with Lane in an old, solid truck felt safe.

"I guess we'll wait to go find food," Ava said offhandedly.

Again, Lane leaned close and reached over her. He popped open the glove compartment. Inside were a few scattered items, like folded papers, a flashlight, some granola bars, and beef jerky packs. "They're fresh if you want anything."

She was hungry, more than she'd first thought, but she didn't want to eat his emergency stash, or road-trip snacks, or whatever they were. "It's fine, I can wait."

She realized she'd echoed what he'd told her earlier about waiting for her to finish practice.

He pulled out his phone, and with a glance, Ava saw that he'd missed calls and texts. "Maybe we can find out how long this will last." He opened up a weather app and tapped on the daily weather report. "Should be passing over within a half hour. You sure you don't want a snack?"

Ava nodded. She slipped off her shoes and drew up her legs so that her heels were propped on the edge of the seat. "Do you live off-campus, then? Since you drove here?"

"Yeah, I rent a room a couple of miles away," Lane said. "Friend of my mom's. She rents out to college students. The connection is why I even looked at the university, and they were the only one to offer me a full ride."

"*Full ride*? Look at you. I guess you really are a smarty pants."

He laughed, and it made her happy to hear it.

"You live off campus?"

"I do." She told him about the apartment she shared with her best friend, Jenni.

"Is she competing tomorrow night?"

"No," Ava said. The AC was working so well now that she actually shivered. "Jenni plays guitar, too. You should meet her—you might have some things in common."

"Jenni? I've heard her practicing before."

"Oh, that's cool. What did you think? She's good, right? Want me to set you up? I mean, if you weren't leaving tomorrow?"

Lane didn't answer for a moment, his blue eyes holding hers. "I don't want to be set up with Jenni. She's a great guitarist, but not my type."

Why was Ava's heart pounding so much? "Oh, so you have a type?"

His smile was instant. "I do now."

He was staring right at her, and she really needed to change the subject. "So, uh, what are your plans, then? You moving back home to Texas until you find a job?"

With a sigh, he said, "Yeah." Then he shook his head.

"What? You don't want to see your family?"

"It's not that," Lane said. "There's a lot going on, and I'm happy to help with things, especially since my brother will be busy with his new kid. Whenever I'm home, though, everyone tries to talk me into staying. Being part of the ranch business. Living in Prosper. Settling down."

"All good stuff," Ava said. "Family, business, a future... right?"

Lane wrapped a hand around the top of the steering

wheel. He was certainly not an indoors man. His ropey forearms and strong hands were witness enough. "Right..."

Ava rested her chin atop her knees. "What do you want to do?"

He glanced at her, then back to the front windshield. "Honestly? Anything outside of Texas. I want to see other places. Experience other things before locking myself down, you know?"

Ava wondered if he'd been reading her journals. "I get it. I mean, it would be fun to be flexible. Travel and work. Not always be in the same location."

His eyes were lighter when he looked at her again. "Exactly. I've applied for some online financial-manager positions. I figured I could get an apartment as a home base, but travel at will. You know, see more than Texas and Arizona."

"Have you been to other states?"

"California and Nevada."

Ava clicked her tongue. "Oh, Lane. You've got to get out more."

"I couldn't agree more," he said. "I just need someone to give me a chance. Get my foot in the door somewhere."

Ava studied him. This guy had the world at his fingertips and he didn't even know it. She'd met him less than two hours ago, but she was already noticing the difference between him and any other guy she'd dated. Or even known.

Something beyond his calm demeanor, his old truck, his straightforwardness, all combined into someone who seemed trustworthy. But could she really trust her first impression? She'd fallen for Brady, after all, and look how that turned out.

Chapter 5

LANE PULLED HIS TRUCK UP to the hole-in-the-wall restaurant. He was pretty sure Ava hadn't been here since it was out of the way, and he'd only seen locals here, no students. The couple of vehicles in the parking lot were covered with a layer of dust, as was everything else in sight. "Do you like Thai food?"

"I think so?" She squinted through the still-dirty windows. The windshield wipers had only marginally cleaned them. "The Thai Place. Sounds good."

Her tone wasn't convincing. "Don't tell me you've never had Thai."

"If I have, I didn't know it. I've had Chinese and Korean, does that count?"

Lane shook his head. "Not exactly. Come on. This is the best Thai I've found in the area." He popped open his door, and just as Ava opened hers, he was on her side of the truck.

He pulled open the door, and as she slid to the ground, he glanced at the sky. At least the dust storm had passed over them, to be replaced by a pale violet sky. Sunset was still a couple of hours away, but the dust storm had moved west, and currently blocked the sun.

"Kind of feels like we're on an abandoned western movie set," he said.

Ava looked around. "Yeah. Eerie. Like everyone has just disappeared."

"Well, hopefully that's not the case," Lane said. "At least the Open sign is turned on."

They walked to the small restaurant. The building had probably once been white, but had settled into a dull yellow. Thanks to the Arizona sun, he guessed.

Once inside, Ava sat across from him in the squeaky red-pleather booth. Lane took off his trusty cowboy hat. A waitress delivered ice water and menus, then left them alone to read them.

"I don't know what anything is," Ava said. "Don't they have pictures?"

"No authentic restaurant has pictures in their menus."

She looked up at him, her brows lifted. "Really?"

Lane chuckled. "I don't know. I just made that up. No pictures at this place, though."

Ava's lips pressed together, and she hummed a little as she looked over the back page of the menu. "I like chicken, but that's not helping me figure out the rest."

"Why don't you try the chicken massaman? That's a good starter for a newbie."

She looked up, then narrowed her eyes. "Is it spicy?"

"It can be," he said. "Do you like spice?"

"Mild is probably the best idea for me."

Lane nodded, holding her gaze longer than was probably necessary. Sitting across from Ava right now was kind of surreal. How had they gone from him listening to her practice in the auditorium to practically being on a date? Their conversations had been casual and humorous so far. Yet he'd told her stuff he hadn't told many people—about his goals and dreams. She hadn't laughed or tried to talk him out of anything—like his family did.

Her brown eyes seemed lighter in the restaurant, and Lane found it hard to look away. Was he staring? He wondered again about Brady—was she heartbroken? She wasn't acting like it, but of course, he didn't know her well enough to figure that out.

Ava closed her menu. "All right, let's go with that. And one of the limeades."

Lane's brows lifted. "That's it? My sisters take at least ten minutes to decide on what to order."

"That seems excessive."

Lane laughed. "It is. Cara sometimes takes longer. She's a chef in California, and not much is up to her standards."

"Oh wow," Ava said. "She must be a good cook, then, if that's her profession."

Lane shrugged. "I wouldn't know. We only see each other at Christmastime, and everything we eat is from my mom's usual recipes. Which are great—don't get me wrong, I'm not complaining."

Ava smirked. "What logical human would complain about good food no matter who fixes it?"

"Exactly."

The waitress returned, and they both gave their orders. When the waitress left again, Ava asked, "So, you have two brothers and how many sisters?"

Lane told her about his siblings: Holt, Knox, Evie, and Cara.

"So Cara is engaged to a famous film producer, and your brother Knox is a bull-rider? That's such a crazy sport."

Yeah . . . Lane usually got that reaction. Without being asked, he opened the photo app on his phone and scrolled back a few weeks to a picture of Knox. He turned the phone and showed Ava.

Her gaze locked onto Knox.

Lane tried not to read into her expression or the way her brown eyes widened.

When she looked up at Lane, she said, "There's a little resemblance. Mostly just the attitude, I think."

"Attitude?"

"Yeah, confidence or something. But your brother looks more cocky than confident."

Lane chuckled. "That would be Knox. He's a . . . complicated guy."

"I gathered that earlier." Ava's eyes danced. "He looks like a guy who's used to the limelight, so bull-riding is probably good for that ego."

"You're extremely observant, Ava." Lane moved to another picture. "That's the whole family."

Ava leaned closer, her dark waves brushing against his wrist. "This is your niece? She's adorable."

"Ruby," Lane said. "Knox and Macie's daughter, but she's got Holt wrapped around her little finger. Well, everyone in the family."

Ava smiled, keeping her eyes locked on the photo. "Who's the redhead?"

"Oh, that's Jana," Lane said. "Knox's fiancée. They knew each other in high school. Everyone was surprised when they started dating again—after Knox and Macie divorced, of course."

Ava nodded. "Complicated, definitely."

"And what about your family? Do you have brothers? Sisters?"

"Nope."

Lane wasn't sure he'd heard her right. "Are you an only child?"

Ava straightened and leaned back in the booth. "All right,

I'll say this fast. Then we can talk about better things. I'm an only child. My dad left when I was eight years old. Found another woman and basically disappeared. My mom worked two jobs to keep things afloat, but it wasn't enough. We ended up at my grandma's house until she passed away, and my mom's siblings fought over everything. My mom said, 'We might not have anything from Grandma, but at least we have memories.' We lived in a one-bedroom after that—so I'm an expert couch sleeper. My mom was busting her butt day and night, and she deserved the bedroom. Our neighbor upstairs taught piano lessons, and I used to fall asleep listening to her play late into the night. Never bothered me. I ended up getting free lessons when I offered to clean her apartment. That turned into long practice hours. By then, it was my senior year in high school, so I was behind everyone else in auditioning for college scholarships. All the spots were filled, and I ended up here in the music program. No scholarship, just depending on student loans to get me through."

She took a breath. "Okay, that wasn't so fast. Any questions?" Her mouth quirked.

There was a lot to unpack, but Lane's first question was, "What's your last name?"

"Sampson."

"And you didn't start playing until you were in high school?"

Ava nodded, then took a sip of her water.

"Wow." He scrubbed a hand through his hair. "Wow. You're something, you know that, Ava Sampson?"

The light in her eyes told him she appreciated his compliment.

"How old are you? I mean, what year are you?"

"I'm twenty-two," she said. "I'll be a senior in the fall."

"You're sticking it out for four years?"

"Gotta get my bachelor's, then I'm hoping to get a master's, too," Ava said. "I'd like to teach. I'm not good enough to tour or join a big symphony."

Lane cleared his throat. "Uh . . . I disagree."

She smirked. It was a cute smirk. "You're sweet, but I'm surrounded by amazing talent every day. Not to mention the competition for jobs as a musician. You have to be extremely talented, have connections, and be lucky."

"Ah, luck," Lane said. "That can be tricky."

"Right?"

The food arrived, and Lane's stomach grumbled. But first he waited until Ava took her first bite of the chicken massaman. She blew on the steaming fork, then ate a mouthful.

When she swallowed and said, "It's good. Great, actually," Lane couldn't be happier.

Why he cared so much, he wasn't sure. He'd ordered the same thing, just with a higher heat level.

"The limeade is excellent," she said after she'd sipped her drink. "Really fresh."

They ate in silence for a few minutes, then Lane asked, "Where does your mom live?"

"Mesa."

"Oh, not far."

"Yeah, I wanted to stay kind of close to home if possible," Ava said. "Plus, out-of-state tuition would be too much without a scholarship."

Lane nodded. He knew. He wouldn't be here without having a scholarship. Now, it was all over. Three and a half years at the same college, and he met Ava on his last day. Ironic. But their majors were pretty opposite, and it seemed she'd had a boyfriend until recently.

"So, when I was listening to you practice earlier, was that Brady who came in to talk to you?"

Ava's brows lifted. "Uh, yeah." She took a sip of her drink.

"Was he bothering you?"

She lifted a shoulder. "He's trying to justify everything, like usual. I saw him with another girl—only flirting, but still. It's not the first time I've seen him do that with other girls. He claims he's being friendly but . . . after what my dad did to my mom, I guess I need to have solid trust with a boyfriend."

Lane nodded.

"And you?" she prompted.

"No girlfriend here—as you overheard. My parents have been harassing me to date in college but . . . well, when my brother Knox met Macie, they got married because of the baby. That all went south because Knox did some stupid stuff. I saw how much his poor choices hurt my parents—the whole family, really—and so I guess I've stayed clear of anything beyond a first date."

Ava set her fork down. "You've only been on first dates in college?"

"Yep."

Ava scrunched her nose. "Are you a player?"

So she was direct. "Not at all. Just . . . didn't meet someone interesting enough to make it to a second date."

"Oh, you're one of *those* guys. Picky. Probably have a dos and don'ts list in your back pocket."

He knew she was teasing, but he didn't want her to think he was either of those things. "No list. I don't want to lead someone on if I already know it won't go anywhere."

Her brows arched. "Well, then, I'm glad *this* isn't a date."

Lane smirked, but inside, his heart had started a slow pound. This *could* be a date. A first date . . . if he weren't leaving tomorrow.

"So, what's your family like?" Ava asked.

He told her some family stories, which were all centered on the ranch and the town rodeo. Ava shared stories about her summers working odd jobs. He couldn't help but laugh when she told him how she was fired three times in the same week.

"None of them were my fault," Ava said.

"It's too much of a coincidence, though," Lane said with a teasing grin. "The constant variable in all the situations was *you*."

She puffed out a breath. "Yeah, you're right. I guess I wasn't cut out to be a janitor in a salon, or a cashier in a tattoo shop, and definitely not a four o'clock in the morning bread maker."

Lane chuckled. "The first summer in college, I went home and worked my family's ranch. Same with the second summer. The last two, I've doubled up on credits to get through faster."

The waitress showed up with the check. Lane snatched it and insisted on paying.

"I thought this wasn't a date," Ava said.

Lane shrugged. "I'm still paying. Sorry."

Ava tilted her head. "I know enough Texan to know that 'sorry' isn't an apology."

Lane replaced his hat and stood. Then he held out his hand. Just being a gentleman, he told himself. Ava took it, and once she was on her feet, he released her hand. He didn't want her to read into anything.

At the front cashier, he paid, then handed Ava one of the wrapped mints. "They're not Thai, but they're still good."

"Oh, okay." Ava unwrapped the mint and popped it into her mouth. "Looks like the dust storm is completely cleared out now."

Lane moved toward the front door, held it open for Ava, then glanced at the horizon. The sun had sunk against the western horizon, and the dust storm had dissipated as if it had never happened, leaving behind an expanse of violet sky and glittering stars. The heat had also calmed down, and the wind was only a whisper.

They walked to the truck in silence, and Lane wished the night didn't have to end so soon. But there was packing to do. Phone calls to make to his family members who'd been texting him. An update to get on Macie and Holt and their baby.

He opened the passenger door for Ava to climb in.

Before she did, she paused. "Do you need help packing?"

He looked down at her, surprised at her offer. When Shelby had offered, the hairs on his neck had stood up. But Ava was a completely different story. Surely, she was being nice, though those brown eyes of hers seemed genuine.

"I'm really good at de-junking, and fitting things into bags and boxes."

"Are you now?"

She nodded. "I'm kind of an organization nut. I'll label your boxes, and tape them up just for fun."

"Fun?"

She was smiling, and he was, too.

"I'm an unconventional girl."

He couldn't agree more. "I don't want to put you out. Besides, do we know each other well enough for you to come over to my place?"

Her eyes twinkled. "I know all about your family, your scholarship, your lack of dating anyone twice, and well, you paid for dinner."

"You don't owe me—"

She put a hand on his chest. That stopped him right there. "I know. I want to help. Maybe as a goodbye present of 'thanks for hanging out with me tonight and keeping my mind off my lame ex-boyfriend.'"

"In that case," Lane said, "I'm happy to be of service." He opened the door wider and motioned for her to climb in.

As she moved toward the bench, he grasped her hand to give her a boost up. The soft warmth of her hand seemed to remain even after he let go.

Chapter 6

Ava scrolled through the texts on her phone as Lane drove them to his apartment on the other side of campus. Her mom had texted, asking about where the toaster was. Ava almost laughed. Her mom was always misplacing things—but the *toaster*? That seemed hard to lose.

Look in the cupboard with the waffle maker, she texted back. It was the only logical thing she could think of.

Next, she opened a string of texts from Brady.

He wasn't giving up. Irritation heated her neck as she read through the sugary sweet texts, the silly GIFs, and the pleadings ending with heart emojis. She must have sighed out loud, because Lane asked, "Is everything okay?"

She looked over at him. She could hardly believe they'd only met a few hours ago. That she was riding in his truck. That she'd offered to help him pack. That she felt so comfortable with him. That she *wanted* to spend more time with him even though he'd be history by tomorrow morning.

"It's Brady. I guess he thinks he can sweet-talk me through texting, and I'll change my mind, then beg him to come back."

"Sweet-talking texts. Hmm. Is it working?"

"Hardly." Ava scoffed. "I refuse to fall for his pretty lines. I refuse to be an easy woman." Maybe that had been too blunt, but she and Lane had had some pretty blunt conversations already. Maybe it was because he'd be leaving tomorrow that it was so effortless to be open with him.

"I get it. I refuse to be an easy woman, too."

"Ha-ha," she deadpanned.

He smiled. "But really, Ava. Are you all right? You're great to offer to help me, but if you need to be somewhere else, I can take you there."

"Don't you want my help?"

He slowed at a traffic light and stopped, the truck rumbling. Darkness had fallen, and the streets were quiet. "I'd love your help, but I don't want to put you out."

Ava didn't like this back and forth. She'd offered. He'd accepted. End of story. "It's your choice, Lane. Maybe I want to stay busy, you know, so I don't get sucked into the world of sweet-talking texts and corny GIFs."

The traffic light turned green, but Lane was still looking at her. "I don't know if I can compete with all that," he teased.

She released an exaggerated sigh. "I'm pretty sure that if you were to compete with Brady in anything, you'd win. Unless it were violin, of course."

"That I can't do." He turned his attention to the intersection and stepped on the gas. "Brady should have appreciated what he had when he had it."

"Dang straight." Ava laughed. "I mean, I *am* quite a catch."

Lane's gaze shifted to her again. Quickly, this time, before he focused once again on the road.

The way he looked at her, even when it was just a glance, sent her stomach spinning. In a good way. In a tempting way. In a way she needed to ignore. Yet, here she was, heading to his place.

Take a Chance

Lane pulled to the side of a double driveway of an older house. He parked on a gravel strip, then turned off the truck. They were in a residential area not far from campus.

"I'll grab your door," Lane said as he popped open his own.

So Ava sat and waited, watching him head around the front of the truck. "So formal," she said, when he opened her door and she slid to the ground.

"Well, when your mother has a sixth sense, you don't want to set her off."

Ava smirked. "You have a good mom, then. But really, you don't have to open the door for me all the time. I'm perfectly capable."

Lane was leading her along the side of the house, then down a set of stairs to a back basement entrance. He put his hand on the knob, then paused to look at her. "You're very capable, Ava, but I'd still like to open your doors. If that's okay with you?"

His low voice rumbled like a deep melody.

Ava nearly sighed. "It's okay with me."

His smile flashed, and he turned the knob, then flipped on a light. She stepped past him into a room that had boxes stacked in one corner. On the other side sat a kitchen table, a couple of chairs, a couch that had seen better days, and an old piano.

"Looks like you've already packed?"

"I've boxed up stuff for donations so far," Lane said, setting his keys on the kitchen table. "I still need to pack up what I'm actually taking with me."

Ava's gaze settled back onto the piano. "Why do you have a piano if you don't play?"

"Guess it's stored down here or something," Lane said. "There's only so many times I can play nursery rhymes, so it mostly collects dust."

Ava walked to the piano and plunked out a short tune. "Ouch. Really needs tuning."

"That's what I thought." Lane joined her. "Either that, or my playing is rusty."

Ava had been alone with Lane for hours, yet right now, she felt very . . . alone with him. Her breathing seemed to increase because he smelled nice, and she really liked his smile, and the way he looked at her and . . . She stepped away.

"Well, do you have a Sharpie? I like to label as I pack."

Lane moved to the kitchen and rummaged through a drawer. "I think this works okay."

Ava tested it out on one of the packed boxes. "Good enough. Now where are we starting?"

"The bedroom," Lane said. "Then the bathroom. Uh, but I'll do that."

Lane led the way to the bedroom. "I'll just bundle up the bedding in the morning, but everything in the closet and dresser drawers can be packed." He set some empty boxes on the queen-sized bed, then opened one of the drawers.

So Ava moved to the closet. It was kind of surreal to be packing up his stuff—his personal stuff. She supposed that movers did it every day.

"Oh, wow, this shirt is really . . ."

Lane chuckled. "You were saying?"

Ava held up a black western-style shirt with white fringes across the front and along the sleeves. "It's really . . . western."

"It's a dress shirt—you know, for a formal event."

Ava lifted her brows. "Do you go to many around here? I mean, you'd certainly stand out if you wore this. Not that you need something extra to stand out."

Lane was walking toward her. The bedroom was already small, and now it seemed even smaller. Warmer, too.

"I haven't worn it the whole time I've been out here." He

took it from her and held it up. "My mom packed it. Thought I'd need it, I guess."

Ava felt a smile push through. "You haven't worn it once? Now, that's a shame."

Lane's blue gaze cut to hers. "How so?"

"Well." Her heart was beating a little too hard. "I'm curious about how you'd look in it. So I was hoping I could see a picture."

Lane rolled his eyes. "You're a tease, Ava." His gaze scanned her face. "But if you're really curious, I could model it for you."

Ava had gone too far. She knew that now. But she'd already dug the hole. "Sure, why not? I mean, then you could at least tell your mom you wore it."

"True." Lane set the shirt on the bed, then started to unbutton the one he was wearing.

"What are you doing?"

"Taking off my shirt so I can try on the fringe."

Ava swallowed against her suddenly dry throat. Even with just three buttons undone, she was having a hard time keeping her eyes on his face.

She turned around.

Lane chuckled. "It's only my shirt."

And they were in his *bedroom*. And going off the size of his forearms and the breadth of his shoulders, she was pretty sure she might swoon if she saw him shirtless.

"What do you think?" he asked.

She looked over her shoulder. He had the fringed shirt on, and the black color made his eyes seem even bluer. She turned fully around and set her hands on her hips. "Well . . . it's a little bit hokey, but it kind of works on you."

"Hokey? What does that mean?"

"I don't know," she said. "Cheesy? But not exactly cheesy."

"You think this shirt is cheesy?"

She held up her thumb and finger, about an inch apart. "A little."

He grabbed her hand and tugged her close. "I'll have you know that this shirt is top quality and top style."

His voice was a growl, but he was grinning.

She put her hand on his chest and pushed against him. "I'll take your word for it."

He released her, but it was too late. His touch had sent fire to every part of her. Ava was toast. She shouldn't have come to Lane's place. She was on the rebound, it seemed, and definitely had her rose-colored glasses on.

"Want me to take a picture?" Lane teased. "Something to remember me by?"

Her cheeks ignited. "Uh, no thanks."

"Suit yourself." He unbuttoned the shirt and shrugged it off.

Ava had forgotten to turn around. So . . . she'd been right. Lane without a shirt wasn't something she'd be forgetting anytime soon, if ever. Was there any spot on his torso he *didn't* have muscle? He folded the shirt and set it into a box, then slipped on his original shirt. It was like he'd forgotten she was in the room, staring at him.

Was she staring? Yes, yes she was.

When Lane looked over at her, she cleared her throat.

"You okay?" he asked. "You look a little . . . hot."

Ugh. She was more than hot. She was an inferno. "I'm fine." She turned to the closet and took down the next shirt. This one she didn't ask about, simply folding it, then setting it in a box.

Lane continued taking things out of the dresser drawers, and after several minutes, Ava had to ask, "So, do you lift weights or something? I mean, you're kind of built. And a business-finance major isn't the most athletic degree."

Lane straightened from the drawer he was unloading. The lift of one eyebrow told her that he saw right through her. "Not weights, at least not the barbell type. I worked weekends on a ranch not far from here. Baling hay mostly. Earned a few bucks for groceries."

"Ah." Ava nodded, then turned back to the closet.

"What about you?"

She looked over her shoulder to see him gazing at her. "Weights? Oh no. Nothing like that. I mean, I'll go jogging a few times a week, but I'm kind of a wimp with everything else. No sports, no riding horses, no hay-baling, and definitely no rodeo."

"I might have guessed that, since you're on the skinny side."

Ava frowned. "I have curves."

His voice seemed to lower. "You do have curves. All I meant was that runners are skinnier than most other people."

She was definitely thinner than her roommate, Jenni, but it wasn't something Ava aspired to. When she was thirteen, a boy had teased her that she looked like a boy.

Ava had been a late bloomer, it seemed. But Lane had definitely checked her out, more than once. Yet, he stayed on one side of the room, and she on the other, while they continued to pack. It was going pretty fast, though, and when Lane finished with the dresser, he said, "I'll be packing up the bathroom. Let me know if you need anything."

Someone knocked on the door just then, and Lane frowned.

"Expecting someone?"

"No. At least I hope I'm not."

This captured Ava's attention, because he'd gone a bit pale.

The knocking started up again.

"Well, aren't you going to answer?" she asked. "I mean, it's pretty obvious you're home. Your truck's out there, and all the lights are on in here."

"Yeah, you're right." He headed out of the bedroom, his back stiff.

This was interesting . . . Ava followed. Too curious for her own good, maybe.

On the other side of the door stood a young woman.

Her red hair was curled about her shoulders, and in her hands she carried two large sacks. "Hi, Lane-y. Brought you dinner." She held up the sacks. "Hope you're hungry."

CHAPTER 7

"SHELBY," LANE SAID, HIS THOUGHTS colliding with a hundred questions. "What are you doing here? H-how do you know where I live?"

Shelby laughed. "Oh, I asked around. I figured someone would know. The college isn't *that* big."

First of all, Lane wasn't hungry; second of all, it was hard enough getting rid of Shelby when they were on campus surrounded by people. But now she had him trapped, at his apartment. It was just them—oh, and Ava in the back room.

An idea clicked into place, but he could only hope Ava would go along with it.

"I'm not all that hungry," he said. "Besides, I'm in the middle of packing."

Shelby's hip cocked. "I can help. In fact, I was planning on it." Her smile widened, then her eyes shifted. "Oh. You have a . . . *girl* over here."

Lane froze. Sure enough, Ava had come into the room. It was just as well, though—he needed her for his plan to work. "Oh, yes. This is Ava." He reached for her hand and hoped she wouldn't tug away.

Shelby might still be on the other side of the screen door, but she didn't miss the fact that he was holding Ava's hand.

Shelby's brow wrinkled. "I thought you didn't have time to date."

"I don't." Lane drew Ava closer to his side. She came easily, but still hadn't said a word. "Ava's a friend, and she's helping me tonight." He squeezed her hand, hoping that she understood he was temporarily using her to get rid of Shelby.

"That's me," Ava said in a cheery voice. "A friend helping Lane pack." She slid her other hand up his arm and leaned into him.

"Thanks, babe," Lane murmured, looking down at Ava with a lazy smile on his face.

She tilted her head and grinned up at him. "You're welcome, hot stuff."

It took all of his willpower to not burst out laughing. Ava's hand moved higher on his arm, resting on his bicep.

He sort of wished they weren't putting on an act. Ava's hand was soft, warm, and she smelled nice.

"So you're just *friends*?" Shelby said in a bright tone. "Are you hungry, Ava?"

Ava turned her head to look at Shelby, then blinked real slow. "No. Lane took me out for Thai food. It was delicious, but I'm stuffed. I couldn't eat another thing for hours and hours."

"Oh." Shelby blinked and lowered her hands.

"I wouldn't feel good about taking the food you brought," Lane continued. "I'll be leaving too early to have anything for breakfast."

Shelby looked from Lane to Ava, then back to Lane. "Well, if you change your mind, I can be here in five minutes." She bit her lip and looked down at where they were still holding hands. Then she whispered, "I think Ava has a crush on you, Lane. You'd better watch out."

Lane held back a laugh, and instead, nodded solemnly. "I'll watch out. Thanks for the warning."

Shelby's smile went bright again. "Oh, since you're moving and all, do you know who's going to be living here next? Will it be a guy? Maybe he'll need a friend? I can give him a campus tour."

"I don't know." Lane tried to keep a straight face. "Sorry."

"Oh, no worries." Shelby laughed. "To think that I thought you might be lonely. I should have known better, Lane-y. A man like you is probably never alone." She lifted her eyebrows, then turned on her heel.

Lane really had no words to that . . . He'd been avoiding Shelby for weeks, but all it took to get rid of her was to have another girl at his side—pretending to be interested.

"Wow. Who was that?" Ava asked in a hushed tone, as if Shelby might still be lurking outside.

"Shelby." Lane looked down at Ava. She was still latched onto his arm, and he wasn't about to remind her of that. "I'm surprised you don't know her. She's quite memorable."

"I'll say." Ava scrunched her nose. "She called you Lane-y. Is that a nickname that you prefer or something?"

Lane groaned. "Please don't ever call me that. Ever. No. It's not a nickname I prefer."

Ava released his arm and folded her own. Smirking, she said, "I'll try to remember that. But wow . . . I don't know how else to describe what just happened. Old girlfriend?"

Lane fake-coughed. "We went on a date. Sort of. Wasn't meant to be a date, but we had coffee together, and it was like opening Pandora's box."

Ava frowned. "I wasn't sure if I should feel sorry for her. Thought maybe she didn't have much common sense or something, but then . . . I changed my mind."

"Oh. What's your conclusion, then?"

"I think she's more of a stalker." Ava crossed to the kitchen table and leaned against it. "I mean, she seemed pretty bright. Eager. A bit too eager, you know."

"Yeah." Lane scrubbed a hand through his hair. "I've tried to turn her down, over and over. Give her plenty of hints without being outright rude. But if you hadn't been here tonight, I don't know how I would have gotten her out of here. *Babe*."

Ava grinned. "Happy to help a dude in distress. I don't think I've ever seen a guy so nervous before."

Lane exhaled. "Yeah. Well . . . thanks again."

"No problem, *hot stuff*." She winked, then headed back to the bedroom.

For a moment, Lane stood in the middle of the room, surrounded by stacks of boxes. He liked her. Ava, not Shelby. Yep. He really liked her. What were the chances that he'd meet her the day—no, hours—before he was leaving?

For the first time in over a year, ever since his buddies all graduated, Lane wished he had another semester here.

"Oh wow. Where did these come from? I thought you said you didn't ride rodeo."

Lane had no idea what Ava was referring to. But he smiled as he walked to the bedroom. He leaned against the doorframe and watched as she held up a well-worn pair of leather chaps.

"I don't ride."

She looked up at him, her smile blooming on her face. Her wavy hair was tossed over one shoulder, and her brown eyes sparkled. "What's the story, then, Lane-y?"

"Don't call me that."

She only grinned. "What? Lane-y? I think it's cute."

"Here, give those to me." He stepped forward, but she backed up, holding them out of reach.

He reached anyway, and she backed up again. So he lunged for them.

She yelped and hopped onto the bed. Before she could scramble to the other side, he caught her ankle. "Hand them over, babe."

She dissolved into laughter, which only gave him the advantage. He tugged the chaps out of her weakened grip, then set them in a box.

Ava slid off the bed, standing on the other side now. "You're really not going to tell me?"

Lane raised a brow. "If you have to know..."

She gave a firm nod, accompanied by a smirk.

"I wore them sometimes." He shrugged. "At the ranch where I helped. Sometimes I rounded up the steers, and well, these protected my nice jeans."

Her brows shot up. "Define *nice* jeans. From what I've packed, everything is well-worn. So I don't know why you're using chaps. They haven't helped much. Not that I'm complaining about your current pair."

He knew she was teasing, but her words still sent fire straight to his stomach. He moved around the bed, and she took a few steps back. There wasn't really anywhere for her to go, though, unless she decided to climb over the bed again.

"I didn't realize that your offer to help would give me so much grief," he said in a low voice.

She tilted her head, meeting his gaze. "Should I shut up?"

"No."

She smiled. He smiled back.

His heart was floating somewhere near the ceiling.

"Well, cowboy," she said, patting his chest.

His knees might have wavered a bit.

"I'm finished in here." She moved past him, and their arms brushed. "Want some help in the bathroom?"

The quarters would be way too tight for the pair of them. The bedroom had already shrunk in size. "Almost finished there. I can take you home, though. You don't have to wait around."

"Oh, you're not getting off that easy," she said, heading out of the bedroom.

"What do you mean by that?" he called after her.

She paused at the doorway and turned. "I want to hear you play that guitar propped up by the piano before I leave. You know, to see how bad you are."

"I don't think so." Lane moved toward her again.

But she moved away before he could reach her. He followed her through the maze of boxes. She made a beeline right for the guitar he'd hauled from Texas and had taken out maybe a dozen times. It was really just a campfire thing he did, but he hadn't been to a lot of campfires here.

She knelt and opened the case, then lifted out the guitar. She settled back on her knees and played a few chords.

"You know how to play?"

She looked up at him, still strumming. "I'm not good, but I'm not bad, either."

"I thought you'd barely learned piano in high school."

She shrugged. "My roommate taught me a few things, but I can only play nursery rhymes."

Lane scoffed. "Let me see that. You're butchering G."

Ava handed it over with a knowing smile. Lane felt set up. She had helped him a lot, though, so he could indulge her a little. He strummed a few chords, then played a simple melody.

"What is that?"

"Nothing really."

He could feel her stare, but he continued to play.

"Did you write it?"

Well, there was no use denying it. Besides, if she liked it, that was pretty cool. "Mm-hmm."

"Lane." Her hand landed on his arm. "What the heck? You write songs?"

"Not technically," he said, switching to another chord. "I don't *write* anything down, and there aren't any words."

She was still staring at him, and her hand was still on his arm, the pressure warming him there.

"I don't think it needs any words," she said. "It's pretty enough without them. Relaxing, you know."

He nodded. Casually. Although inside, he was reveling in her compliment. He hadn't played much around other people. Mostly for himself, unless it was at a campfire.

Ava rose to her feet and sat on the nearby piano bench. Maybe she was bored already? Or did she have a compulsion to play every piano she saw? She played a soft melody, and Lane quickly realized it was mirroring his own song.

He switched keys and sped up. She did, too.

Looking over her shoulder, she said, "Throw it at me. I'll keep up."

So he did. He played through a bunch of stuff he'd either made up over the years or improvised from other songs. Ava followed along like they were playing a duet. Sometimes, she even anticipated his chord change or switch in mood.

Lane rose from the couch and moved toward her. Leaning against the piano, he caught her gaze as she looked up. Her smile was like a delicious summer day, with nothing on the horizon but a cold glass of sweet lemonade.

When he sped up, she did, too. When he slowed down, she followed, until he strummed a conclusion. She added a few chords for flair on the piano, then she stood and clapped.

Lane laughed.

"Wow," she said, her face glowing. "That was the most fun I've ever had doing a duet."

His brows lifted. "I don't even know what to call it."

She moved out from the piano bench. "I don't know, either, but it was brilliant. Or at least it felt brilliant. What would you call it?"

"Uh, you're brilliant. I didn't know you could improvise and follow along like that."

She shrugged. "I've done it a little, but never with guitar, or with random songs that you say you didn't write."

"Nothing's written down," he said. "You can check every box."

She smirked. "Well, Lane Prosper, I have to disagree with you."

"About what?" The edges of his mouth dipped.

"You're really good on the guitar," she said. "If you ever change your mind about pursuing music, I think you'd do well."

Lane chuckled. "You're sweet, Ava. But I think I'm set. My degree—"

"Oh hush," Ava said, setting her hand on his chest. "You're talented. At least admit it. You don't have to go through a career change or anything, but you're a hot-stuff guitar player."

Lane gazed into her brown eyes. They were only inches apart, and this close up, he could see golden flecks. "Hot stuff, huh?"

Her mouth curved. "Yeah." Her hand moved up a little. Over his heart. Her fingertips at his collarbone. "Too bad you're leaving in the morning." Her voice was soft, nearly a whisper.

He set his hand over hers. Through her hand, he could feel the thump of his heart beneath. "Why's that?"

She exhaled. Her smile was gone, replaced by seriousness. "I think I would have liked to go out on a second date with you. That is, if you'd be willing to break your one-date streak."

Something sighed through him. Something warm and light, but he couldn't quite grasp it and make it stay. An ache came instead. Why did he have to meet her *today*? Why couldn't it have been a year ago? Or even a month ago?

"I'd break it," he said. "That is, if I were staying."

Her gaze seemed to deepen, then her fingers curled into his shirt, and she lifted up on her toes.

Something in the back of his mind told him what was happening, but it was hard to believe it really would. When she pressed her mouth against his, there was no denying it.

She pulled away quicker than lightning; he'd barely had time to close his eyes.

"Sorry about that," she said in a breathless tone. "I didn't mean . . . I shouldn't have . . ."

He set the guitar on the ground, then he cradled her face with both hands. "I'm not sorry," he whispered, before he bent down for a second kiss.

Her fingers wrapped around his forearms as she held onto him, kissing him back.

Heaven, he thought, was supposed to be all that. But this, right here kissing Ava, was heaven.

Neither of them moved any closer, but let the kiss become the focus between them.

Nothing about this time with Ava had been planned, or could have been predicted, but whatever paths of fate had brought them to this point, in this moment, Lane would never forget even one second.

Chapter 8

THE HEAT COMING OFF OF Lane while he kissed her only added to her own. Ava knew this kiss would be the one and only chance she had with this man, so she was making it count.

She sighed into his kiss, wanting more. He seemed to understand, and his hands angled her face as he kissed her deeper. She opened to him, let him in, and tasted him as much as he was tasting her. Then his fingers were buried in her hair, and his mouth pressed to her jaw, his lips warm and firm.

Goose pimples erupted along her skin. She was having a hard time catching a full breath. But she didn't want to separate from him, not yet. She ran her hands up his arms until they reached his shoulders. He was so solid, warm, steady. She could lose herself in his touch if she allowed it.

And she couldn't allow it. She shouldn't have kissed him, shouldn't have started this. But he was so . . . delicious.

"Lane," she whispered.

He lifted his head. His blue eyes were a murky gray, slightly unfocused. "Ava," he whispered back, the edges of his mouth lifting. "Where have you been the past four years?"

She exhaled. "Treading water."

He leaned in again, his mouth finding hers. But this kiss was lighter, softer, slower. It was as if they both knew nothing could go further between them than it already had. She stepped closer and wrapped her arms about his neck, just holding him.

Lane's arms encased her as he buried his face against her neck, his breath warm on her skin.

Her heart was racing as fast as his, and they seemed to breathe in tandem. "I should go," she murmured. "You're too tempting, and I'm not that kind of girl."

His hands moved up her back. Fresh goosebumps skittered along her arms.

"I don't leave until sunrise."

She smiled, even though he couldn't see it. "Yeah. That's what I mean. Too tempting." When she loosened her hold on him, he drew away, and their gazes locked.

"Ava..."

"Hush." She put her finger on his lips to stop whatever he was going to say. Maybe she shouldn't have kissed him, but she didn't regret it. She *would* regret it if she didn't leave now, though, because it would only get harder.

She lowered her hand, then stepped out of his arms, putting needed breathing space between them. "I'll get an Uber," she said.

Lane's brows tugged together. "I can take you home, no problem."

"It's okay," she rushed to say. Her face was heating up, her body was still warm, and she was starting to feel foolish. She'd been too impulsive. "I don't want to ruin this night. If I haven't already."

Lane grasped her hand, his fingers threading through hers. He didn't pull her closer or try to kiss her. "You didn't ruin this night, Ava. I think it's the best night I've had in four years."

She smiled at that. "And four years ago?"

He squeezed her fingers then let go. Lifting both hands, he said, "Look, I'll keep my hands to myself, and I'll get you home safe and sound."

"Okay." Ava bit her lip. She wanted to stay. Or more accurately, she wanted *him* to stay. Find a job nearby. Or maybe she could tell him that he should get an MBA—stay in school longer, be on campus.

But all that was ridiculous and wishful thinking. They'd literally known each other for, what, six hours? Seven?

She hadn't looked at her phone in a while, and there was no wall clock in sight.

Lane snatched up his keys from the kitchen table, then put on his cowboy hat. When he held the door open for her, she knew the night had really, finally, come to an end.

She walked through the doorway, forcing each step forward. Folding her arms to hold herself together, she walked to the truck.

Lane opened the door, and she climbed in, keeping herself at a safe distance. Lane had been right. This night had been perfect. She just hated to see it end.

When Lane started the truck, she wanted to reach over and grab his hand. Link their fingers. Feel his warmth and strength against her skin. But she kept her gaze out the window, away from his profile.

She told him where to turn, and then where to stop in front of her place.

Before she could tell him not to worry about walking her to the main doors of the apartment building, he'd hopped out.

"You don't have to walk me to my apartment," she said when he opened the truck door.

He held the door open anyway, just standing there, his gaze on her. Deep and thoughtful.

She sighed, then slipped to the ground. She walked toward the front doors with Lane walking next to her, his hands shoved in his front pockets.

It was just as well. More touching by him would only make this more agonizing.

It wasn't lost on her that the rush of emotions she was having around Lane should have been something she'd felt with Brady, who'd been her boyfriend for months. But nothing about Brady even compared to Lane.

It seemed that the heart couldn't choose.

This brought her thoughts up short. Was her heart already involved? Impossible. Or it should be impossible. And yet . . .

"I guess this is it?" Lane said, his voice a low rumble. "You walk into those doors, back to your life. And I head out to another state."

Ava slowly turned to face him.

His gaze hadn't left her.

"This is it." Her throat felt raw for some reason. "For whatever it's worth, I enjoyed spending time with you. And I hope you get a killer job, see the world, and find everything you're looking for. But if you're ever back in town, look me up."

"Will do." He gave a curt nod. "Good luck in your competition. I hope you kick everyone's butts. You deserve it."

"Thanks." She felt completely out of breath, even though she was standing still. "Drive safely, okay?"

Another nod. "Don't let Brady talk you into anything."

At this, she smiled. Brady was so, so far in the past. Like eons. "I won't."

Lane lifted a hand and ran his fingers down her hair.

"Play that song," he whispered. Then he dropped his hand and stepped back.

She couldn't read the depth of his eyes in the moonlight. But she couldn't let him go, let him leave forever, without one more hug.

She stepped forward and threw her arms about his neck. He crushed her against him in a fierce hug. Their hearts beat wildly together for a full minute.

Then it was over. He released her and she turned, tugged open the door, and retreated to the safety of the dark hallway. Where no one could see her tears.

Her apartment was dark and quiet. Either Jenni wasn't home yet or she was asleep. Ava checked the bedrooms. No one was about. Well, it was still early. Not even eleven p.m. At Jenni's bedroom, Ava paused. She had a couple of guitars, and the one in the corner was an older one like Lane's.

Ava crossed the room and picked up the guitar, then sat on the edge of the bed and plucked out a few chords. She wasn't good enough on the guitar to pick out the song Lane had played. He was one talented man, and he didn't even know it. But she sensed that if Lane Prosper put his mind to something, he'd probably accomplish it.

Ava's phone dinged.

Had Lane already texted her? They'd exchanged numbers, but not any promises. Maybe things between them didn't have to completely end. A little long-distance flirting? But when she pulled her phone out of her back pocket, she sighed. Brady was not letting up.

Apparently, he'd texted Jenni to find out what Ava was up to tonight. *I just wanted to check in on you, make sure you're okay. Hope you don't mind.*

It was such a leading question that Ava cringed.

She switched to Jenni's contact and typed out: *What did you tell Brady about me?*

Take a Chance

Seconds later, Jenni replied. *Nothing. Told him I hadn't seen you.*

Okay, thanks. Ava paused. *I'm probably going to block him. He's not letting up.*

What's going on? If he's being creepy, we should report him!

One thing about Jenni was that she had a flair for the dramatic. It wasn't like Brady was stalking her or anything. Was he? *He's just being annoying. I just don't want to deal with it anymore.*

I don't blame you. I mean, I never really liked him. Too flirty.

Ava stared at the screen. Her own roommate and friend thought Brady was too flirty . . . Why hadn't Jenni said anything? *What do you mean? Was he flirty with you?*

Uh, yeah. Remember I said something that one time?

Ava drew a blank. *Where are you?*

Coming up the stairs.

Ava stood and made it to the front door by the time Jenni arrived. Her short pixie haircut had pink streaks in it this week. She changed hair color a lot. It was something Ava loved about her.

"What the heck, Jenni?" Ava said. "I don't remember you telling me Brady was flirty with you."

Jenni set a sack of fast food on the counter, then dug through it and pulled out some fries. "Want some?"

"No thanks," Ava said. "Spill."

Jenni perched on the kitchen table and popped a fry into her mouth. "Okay, so remember when you guys were going to that Easter concert and you found a rip in your dress? So you went into your bedroom to change into something else? You were running late, and you didn't have time to fix the rip?"

Ava remembered. But instead of thinking of the fun night

they had together, her stomach felt like she'd swallowed a rock. "What did Brady say to you?"

"It wasn't really what he *said*." Jenni picked up another fry. "It was more of what he *did*."

Ava exhaled. "Okay . . ."

"Well, I was fiddling around with one of my guitar pieces, and he sat by me. Like really close. His knee kept bumping mine as he tapped his foot to the song I was playing." Jenni scrunched up her nose. "It was way too much in my personal space, and he was whisper-talking to me like he didn't want you to know we were talking."

"And you told me this?"

"Yeah, the next day." Jenni frowned. "You really don't remember? I said that your boyfriend needed to learn the three-foot rule."

Ah. It was coming back to Ava. She'd laughed and told her roommate that Brady was just a hugger. And he was. But sitting so close to Jenni wasn't cool at all. "Sorry."

"Oh, you were smitten," Jenni said. "And I figured that I'd misread the situation. I mean, Brady hugs everyone he sees, so you know . . . I wrote it off as that."

Ava nodded. She'd made excuses for him, too. Over and over. "I'm still sorry. I should have seen the signs—they were probably there all along."

Jenni moved off the table and held out the sack to Ava. "Take the fries. There's too much, and I hate fast-food leftovers. It's just going to end up in the garbage."

"I'm really not hungry."

Jenni's brows shot up. "That's a first. You always call dibs on leftovers."

"Yeah, but I ate at a real restaurant tonight. Thai food."

"So you spent your entire food allowance already?" Jenni moved to the fridge and yanked open the door. "I'll save it for you, then. You'll just complain about starving tomorrow."

Jenni was teasing, but not fully. Ava was broke, all the time, so food was usually the one thing she couldn't splurge on. She ate as cheaply as possible, then was happy to take leftovers off anyone's hands.

"No, I didn't pay." *Oops.* Too late to take that comment back.

Jenni spun around. "What? Did you go out on a date?"

"Oh my gosh, Jen, you don't need to yell." She didn't know whether to laugh or be mortified.

Jenni grasped Ava's arms. "I want all the tea, right now. Does Brady know? Who's the guy? Where did you go? Do I know him? Is he hot?"

"Stop," Ava said with a laugh. "It was a one-time thing. We got food and hung out a little. I actually helped him pack because he graduated today and moves tomorrow."

Jenni's eyes had widened comically. "Who is this man? I want his full name. Description. Everything. Because you are blushing, Ava."

Ava put her hands to her cheeks. She'd lost count of how many times she'd blushed since meeting Lane today. "It's nothing, really. I'll never see him again anyway."

But Jenni wouldn't let up, so Ava confessed everything. Well, except the kiss. That, she was keeping all to herself.

Chapter 9

When Lane's alarm went off, he dragged his eyes open. No way it was morning. But yes, his stripped bedroom was already light with the morning sun. With a groan, he sat up. It was almost seven a.m.—an hour later than he'd wanted to start. How many times had he hit snooze? It had done nothing to make his headache feel better.

He'd gotten some texts after midnight of Macie's new baby. Everything had gone well, and mom and baby were great. A nice relief. But that still hadn't helped him in the sleep department.

Yeah . . . he'd stayed up way too late finishing up the packing, and then he spent a couple of hours tossing and turning. Wondering why the fates in his life had played such a terrible joke on him.

First, he was perfectly qualified for an excellent position with a financial-planning firm, yet he had no job offers. Second, he'd dated randomly for the past four years, and never, not even once, met someone he was interested in like he was Ava.

Why . . . why . . . why?

Well, it couldn't be helped. Stewing over it for hours last

night hadn't presented any solutions or enlightenment. It was what it was.

And he had a thirteen-hour drive ahead of him where he could analyze everything to death.

Lane headed to the kitchen. He drank down some water with a couple of ibuprofen that were luckily in a box Ava had labeled. Just seeing her handwriting brought back all the memories from the day before. The auditorium. The dust storm. The Thai food. The packing. Shelby's appearance. Ava playing the piano while he strummed his guitar. Their kiss. Her goodbye hug.

Lane wiped a hand over his face. He had to get out of here. Had to move on. Move forward.

It didn't take him long to load all the boxes into his truck, but by the time he was finished, the Arizona sun was plenty warm. His first stop was the Salvation Army, where he donated the stuff he didn't want following him wherever he ended up. His load significantly lighter, he turned onto the main road.

He should be turning right, but instead, he turned left—toward campus. A farewell drive-by, he guessed. Maybe he'd see her, maybe he wouldn't.

The campus was quiet since the semester was over, and those moving out were probably sleeping in longer than Lane. Without second guessing himself, Lane turned onto the street where he'd taken Ava last night. He slowed as he passed by her apartment, wondering if one of the cars parked outside was hers. Wondering which windows belonged to her place. Wondering if she was still asleep. Wondering if she'd slept as poorly as he had.

No one was out who looked like the dark-haired woman he couldn't stop thinking about.

So he continued on, turning back onto the main road that

would take him to the freeway—straight through Arizona and on to Texas.

He turned up the music on the radio, drowning out his thoughts, keeping his mind off what he shouldn't be dwelling on.

His phone rang a few minutes after he hit the freeway.

Lane turned off the radio and tapped the speaker button on his phone since he didn't have his earbuds in. "Holt? How's it going?"

"Hey, man," Holt said in a tired voice. "You heading home?"

"Yep. How's the baby? And Macie?"

"Doing good." Holt exhaled. "They should be coming home this afternoon. Ruby has been up since five this morning getting everything ready."

"I'm sure she's been real helpful," Lane said with a chuckle. The little girl was the apple of everyone's eye, and no matter how tired Holt was, he'd never be mad at her for being excited about her little brother.

"Real helpful," Holt said with a scoff. "She just fell asleep. Mom's coming over so I can go back to the hospital."

"Well, I'm glad it's all going well, even though you've missed a lot of sleep." Lane couldn't stifle his own yawn.

"You're sounding tired, bro," Holt said. "Up late packing? Last minute, as usual?"

"Something like that."

"Uh-oh."

Lane slowed so a sports car could cut in front of him. Someone was in a hurry this morning. "What?"

"You regretting coming home?"

"No." Lane wasn't regretting heading home—this week. But he didn't want to get roped into staying too long. "I said I'd help, and I will. Plus, I want to see the family, especially the baby. What are you naming him?"

"Lucas Rex."

"Ah. I like it." Rex after their dad, but Lucas was a new name. "No Holt in there?"

Holt seemed to hesitate. "Maybe the next kid. I didn't want our first baby together to, uh, you know, be an insult to anyone."

"Yeah, I get it." Lane shook his head, though. Macie and Holt were way too good to Knox. Yeah, everything was patched up now, but Lane thought Macie and Holt didn't need to walk on eggshells anymore around their other brother. The man who was Macie's first husband, and Ruby's father. "You talked to him yet?"

"Nah." Holt released a breath. "I texted him last night, the same time I texted you. No reply yet."

Lane nodded. Knox would reply when he was good and ready. He'd always been that way. Walked through life to the tune of his own melody. His fiancée, Jana, had been good for him, though. And everyone in the family liked her—probably even better than they liked Knox.

"Well, send more pictures," Lane said. "And best of luck to Macie and Lucas."

"Hang on there, bro," Holt said. "What's up? How are the interviews going?"

"Nothing's changed since the last time I updated you," Lane said. "Although I might do some searching in Arizona." The second he said it, the more he liked the idea. Not because of... well, Ava, but because... "I mean, an Arizona university is now my alma mater, so maybe that will give me a foot in the door."

"Huh. Maybe."

Lane knew his brother wouldn't be enthusiastic with anything outside of the Prosper city limits.

"Oh, it looks like Macie's calling," Holt said suddenly. "Catch up later."

"Sure, good luck with everything."

The call disconnected.

Lane turned the radio back on. It was a series of commercials, so he switched stations. Something pop-ish came on, not his favorite. So he switched again. Classical music. Well, no one else was in his truck to give him a hard time. Besides, he was pretty sure that if Ava were here, she'd be pleased.

He smiled at that thought. And he kept smiling. What he'd told Holt was starting to ring more and more true. Working somewhere local to the college might give him a start on his career. Then, he could move on from that. He wondered what Ava's opinion would be.

Nah . . . Too far-fetched. Too presumptuous.

And if there was one thing Lane wasn't going to do, it was put restrictions on job opportunities. He'd come this far . . .

Lane drummed his fingers along the steering wheel as an hour passed in his drive. His phone rang again.

"Hey, Evie," he said. His little sister was back in Prosper, too, after vowing never to live in a small town again. But dating Carson Hunt had changed her mind about all of that.

"Sorry about the phone tag yesterday," Evie said. "Congrats on graduating. Didn't think you had it in you."

"Ha-ha," Lane deadpanned. "If you can survive college, then I definitely can. Piece of cake."

"Oh, whatever," Evie said. "I have a whole string of texts from you complaining about your statistics class."

"Yeah, well, that was then. This is now."

"Oh? Am I going to be seeing a new and improved Lane Prosper tonight?"

Lane chuckled. "I guess you'll be the judge of that."

"Did you see the pics of Lucas? He's so darling."

"Whoa. Evie Prosper is baby hungry? Has the world ended and I don't know it yet?"

"Shut up. You're gonna be in love in two seconds flat."

Lane smiled even though his sister couldn't see him. "So you gotta see him already?"

"Yeah, duh." She cleared her throat. "Carson was pretty nervous to hold him, but it was so cute when he did."

"You are so smitten."

For once, his sister didn't argue, and that's when Lane knew the two must be getting serious.

"Well, Mom's counting down the hours until you get here," Evie said. "What time you driving in?"

Lane glanced at the clock on the dash. "About ten tonight? I've only been on the road for an hour."

"Late start? I thought you said you were heading out at six."

Yeah... that was before Ava. Before a lot of things. "Was up late looking at pictures of my favorite nephew."

"Funny. All right, bro, see you tonight, then."

"See you."

Lane hung up. Talking to Evie was always refreshing. Not like Holt, who liked to dig and dig. His other sister, Cara, hadn't called, and that was fine. Her famous film-producer fiancé had a young daughter, and Cara had recently opened up her own restaurant. She was crazy busy, and the text from her was about what he expected. There'd been a text a few days ago from Knox, and truthfully, it was all Lane expected from him. And he was fine with it. The man was busy and inside his own head most of the time. It was how it was.

Like much of life. You just had to accept the facts and deal with them in your own way. You couldn't put your own expectations on someone else or you'd always be disappointed.

Before Lane could turn the radio back on, another phone call came in, from a number he'd saved in his phone last week.

Johnson and Associates. He hated to answer it when he was driving, knowing the rumble of the truck could be heard in the background. But fumbling with his earbuds right now probably wasn't safe, either.

He pressed the speaker button. "This is Lane Prosper."

"Oh, hello. This is Meredith Johnson. Thanks for picking up."

"No problem, Ms. Johnson. Just a head's up. I'm driving to Texas, but I'm hands-free with the phone. Sorry about the background noise."

"That's all right. Can you hear me okay?"

"Sure thing, ma'am."

She paused. "Yes, well, I'm calling with good news. We've decided to hire you as an assistant to our finance manager. He's retiring in about nine months, and the idea is if all parties are happy, then you'd replace him."

Lane released a slow breath. "Wow." He paused. "Oh, did I say that aloud? I mean, thank you, ma'am, that's amazing news."

"I thought you'd be pleased."

"Well, I am," Lane said. "I'm honored. Truly."

He should just accept on the spot. It was a good job. Yeah, it was in North Carolina, but the benefits were good, and even though he'd be an assistant at first, the pay would set him up in an apartment. Probably could afford payments on a new truck, too. Instead, though, he said, "I'm really excited about this offer and future potential as well. How long do I have before I give you my answer?"

This was something he'd been taught in a careers course. Be grateful, but not too eager. Don't make big decisions in a rush. Ask for time, then look at all the pros and cons.

Ms. Johnson seemed to hesitate. Maybe she'd expected him to accept on the spot. "Well, how about a week? I realize this is a big decision—moving across the country, and all."

"Yes, ma'am, it is," Lane agreed. "I'm very grateful for the time, and if I know my answer beforehand, I'll reach out then."

"All right," she said. "Well, I hope you have a nice day. Drive safe, and all."

After Lane hung up, he drove in silence for several miles. Why wasn't he jumping out of his skin with excitement? If he'd received this phone call twenty-four hours ago, he would have sent a text to his family right away telling them the good news. He would have been googling apartments and pricing out what he'd need to buy for one.

Instead, the offer felt like a weight. Yeah, he was flattered, but that's all it felt like—flattery. Maybe he was more tired than he thought. He just needed to get through this drive and clear his head.

Lane turned the radio back on. It was still on the classical music station. He could identify several of the songs now. His fingers tapped the steering wheel as the notes climbed into a crescendo with the full power of an orchestra behind the melody.

It was breathtaking.

A few hours later, the light on his dash came on telling him that he was low on gas. Oh, that's what he'd planned to do yesterday before he became sidetracked by all that was Ava.

Even as he drove, he could picture her smile. He could hear her teasing. He could feel her hug. Wow. He missed her. Crazy stuff. She was probably awake by now. Maybe even heading off to rehearse.

He took the next exit off the freeway, then pulled into a gas station. While he filled up at the pump, he checked his phone for any texts. There was one from his mom that he must have missed when he was on the phone with Evie.

Drive safe, son. Can't wait to see you.

He wrote back. *Thanks, Mom. Love you.*

He pressed send, then headed into the gas station to grab a drink. He browsed the glass-door refrigerators. There was a limeade—"fresh squeezed," it said, just like Ava liked. Although Lane doubted it was as fresh as it had been at the Thai restaurant. He opened the glass door and took it out, then grabbed his usual cola.

Walking to the register, he set them on the counter. The fifty-something clerk, wearing a matching shirt and ballcap with the gas station logo on them, said, "Oh, that's good stuff. My wife's favorite."

Lane nodded. "Haven't tried it myself. Looks good, though." He paid, then headed out of the gas station. Once he was in the truck and turned on the engine, the radio came blaring on. The classical music made him wonder if Ava was nervous. Maybe he should text her a good luck message? Or would that be crossing the line? Make things awkward?

Lane sat for a minute in the truck, thinking, until someone tapped their horn behind him. It seemed this gas station had suddenly gotten busy. He put the truck into drive and pulled out, then stopped at the light at the corner. Heading right would take him east into Texas. Heading left would take him back to campus. Four hours away.

When the light turned green, Lane flipped on his left blinker.

Chapter 10

AVA HELD THE DOWNWARD DOG pose for another full minute. Then, aching in more than one limb, she moved into a sitting position and let her head fall forward. She loved this yoga class, but her mind wasn't in the right place to really find her zen this afternoon.

She could probably blame the competition in a few hours, but she knew better than that. She hadn't been able to stop thinking about Lane Prosper. He was halfway to Texas by now, maybe farther. There had been multiple times during the day that she'd almost texted him, but hadn't. What would she say anyway that wouldn't end up falling flat? She could just imagine their text thread.

How's the drive?
Good. Lots of sun. Good luck tonight.
Thanks.

Then what? They wouldn't see each other again. They'd had fun yesterday, yes, and it had been nothing but good for Ava. She realized quite a few things about herself and what had been broken in her relationship with Brady. She'd be seeing him tonight. Jenni said she'd be staying close to Ava, even though she wasn't competing. And it was Jenni who'd dragged her to yoga in the first place.

But it had done nothing to relax her mind.

After the class, she and Jenni headed back to their apartment to start getting ready. Ava pulled out her standard concert dress. Black velvet, low-cut back, and flared at the knees. Her phone rang as she was touching up her makeup.

For a second, her pulse leapt, and she wondered if maybe Lane had decided to call her. To wish her luck? But it was her mom's number lighting up the screen.

"Hey, Mom."

At her mom's coughing, Ava held the phone away from her ear for a moment. "Mom, are you okay?"

"It's just a dang cold," her mom said, clearing her throat. "Started out as a tickle this morning, now I keep having coughing—"

Again, her mom coughed several times.

"—fits. Oh, Ava, I don't think I should come tonight. I'm so disappointed."

"It's fine," Ava said. "I hope you feel better soon. That cough sounds nasty. Did you turn on the humidifier?"

"Not yet, but I'm going to," her mom said. "Thanks, honey. And I'm sorry again."

"Just get better," Ava said. "I'll bring you soup tonight if you want."

"Oh, don't you worry about that." More coughing. "Call me after the competition. I'll be waiting up to hear everything."

When Ava hung up with her mom, she pushed away the sting of disappointment. It wasn't that her mom hadn't missed some of her performances; it was just that in college, she didn't get to see her that often.

"Ready?" Jenni's voice sailed down the hallway. She was always ready early, and Ava felt rushed in order to catch up.

Take a Chance

"Almost," Ava said. Her phone dinged. Again, her heart leapt. But she groaned when she saw that it was Brady who'd texted her.

Can't wait to see you tonight. Good luck.

Now, why couldn't it have been Lane? She didn't want to see Brady, and she didn't want to feel like she had to text him back a good luck message as well. They'd be competing against each other. Of course, Brady didn't need the money from the competition, but that didn't stop him from entering. He just wanted to prove his talent.

Brady was an extremely talented violinist. But now, knowing him as she did, she realized he used his talent to get his way with people. Not to bring them joy in music, but to bring himself acclaim and attention.

Ava slipped on her black heels. A final glance in the mirror told her she was as ready as she'd ever be. She'd twisted her hair into a low chignon and put on more makeup than she usually wore so she wouldn't be too washed out on stage.

"Looking hot," Jenni said from the doorway.

Ava looked over at her roommate. Jenni wore a strappy red dress, silver stilettos, and she'd added red streaks to her hair. "You're the hot one. Red hot."

Jenni laughed. "We'll both knock 'em dead. Now, let's hurry."

"It doesn't start for an hour."

"I want front row seats."

Ava shook her head. "You're nuts." Her phone dinged again. This time, she wasn't going to look at it.

"Brady?" Jenni asked as they headed down the hallway.

"Yep."

"Block him, Ava, I'm serious."

She paused at the top of the stairs, then pulled out her

phone. Sure enough, Brady had texted her. *What time are you heading over? I can pick you up on the way.*

She scowled. "It's like he doesn't know we're broken up. He's completely ignoring everything I've told him." She clicked on the contact. "That's it. I'm blocking him."

"Good choice." Jenni slung an arm over her shoulders, and they headed out of the apartment.

The sun was on its way to setting, painting the sky pink and pale orange by the time they arrived at the music hall. The last time Ava had been here, she'd met Lane.

Heading in through the doors, Ava felt a pang deep in her stomach. He hadn't reached out. Yeah, he was driving, but surely he'd stopped to get gas. Maybe she was overthinking it. Or maybe she shouldn't be thinking about him at all. There'd been no promises or commitments between them. And it was probably good that Lane had gone cold turkey on any texting. Made it easier in the long run.

"Are you going to warm up?" Jenni asked.

Ava paused, realizing she'd turned down the wrong hallway. "Oh, yeah. Sure."

Jenni studied her. "You've been off all day. I thought it was just nerves, but now I'm not so sure. Are you having second thoughts about Brady but don't want to tell me?"

Ava's mouth fell open. "Not at all. I'm fine. Really. Just nervous, like you said."

Jenni folded her arms. "Then it's that cowboy. I should have known. Have you been texting him?"

Letting out a breath, Ava shook her head. "No. Nothing from him. I mean, I expected that."

"But when it's really been nothing, you've second-guessed yourself?"

"Yep. Dumb, huh?"

"No. I get it. Remember me and Clint last year?"

Clint had been her on-again, off-again boyfriend for months. It had driven Ava nuts.

"Yeah, I remember. You were only happy when *you* were mad at him, not the other way around."

Jenni winced. "That about sums it up. Not a good relationship, that's for sure." She rubbed Ava's shoulder. "Hey, you need to forget about the men in your life for a few hours. This night should be about you. Your future, you know. Go out there and crush it. Show everyone what you, Ava Sampson, are made of."

Ava stared at her friend, then gave her a fierce hug. "You're right. And that was the best pep talk ever."

Jenni laughed as she hugged Ava close. "Now, go get warmed up. Do you want me with you in case Brady comes into the piano room?"

"No, go get your front row seat." Ava smirked. "I can practically see you're about to go feral."

Jenni hugged Ava again, then hurried off, leaving her in the hallway alone.

This was it. From this point on, it was just Ava and the piano. If she could perform to her best, she had a real shot at winning. Then her future would be secured at the university. And she'd graduate with far less student loan debt.

She strode along the hallway until she reached the piano room. She was the only one here at the moment, thank goodness. Without the ability to reserve warmup time, the place would be a free for all. Ava knew there were two other pianists who'd entered the competition. She hoped to get a warmup in before anyone else came in.

Ava sat at the piano and ran through her usual series of scales. She'd been tempted to play the piece that Lane had loved so much, but it truly wasn't ready. She could put the same passion into her regular number—it was listed on the program anyway. Not that she couldn't announce a different piece, but she didn't want to draw that type of attention to herself.

So she ran through her number once, taking her time to make sure every technical aspect was correct. Then, the room still empty, she ran through the number a second time, adding in emotion to every line and every stanza. She finished with a flourish, then held the final chord for a full fifteen seconds.

"Bravo!" someone said, clapping.

The hairs on her neck stood up, and Ava looked over to see Brady.

He walked into the room, still clapping. The smile on his face wasn't genuine, though. It was . . . angry?

Oh. Maybe he'd realized she'd blocked his number.

"Thank you," she said simply, then turned back to the piano and began another set of scales. Something mind-numbing. Something that would drive him out of the room.

But he didn't leave. Instead, he rested a palm on the edge of the piano, placing him only a couple of feet from her.

She could see him from her peripheral vision, but didn't meet his gaze. The scales were more choppy than usual, and she attributed that to Brady's presence. Not that she was intimidated, or nervous, but she was annoyed. She felt harassed. How many times did she have to push him away, tell him no?

As she continued to play, and he continued to stand there, as if he were lording over her, she felt the anger grow. So what if she'd blocked him? She had every right to decide who got to contact her or who didn't. She didn't even need to explain herself.

When she came to the end of the set of scales, she changed keys and started over.

"Ava."

Brady's voice was quiet, but he might as well have shouted it. She flinched, and the knot in her stomach tightened.

"Ava."

She finally stopped playing and looked up. "Can whatever you want to say wait? I'm warming up, and you probably should be warming up, too."

He tilted his head.

She used to love those green eyes of his, but now they seemed cold and calculating. Also, he was scrawny compared to Lane Prosper. Not that she should be comparing anyone to a man she'd only spent a few hours with, but the difference was noticeable. Brady was scrawny and pale. Green eyes, pale skin, dark hair. All kind of... vampirish.

She had the sudden, inane urge to laugh. How had she been attracted to this man? How had she thought she was falling in love with him? How had she thought he could complete her in any way?

Since he hadn't answered, she began to play again.

That's when Brady reached out a hand and grasped her wrist.

Ava tugged her hand away with a gasp. Then she rose and backed away from the piano. "Don't touch me, Brady. Don't follow me. Stop texting and calling me. We're over. How many times do I have to tell you that?"

He didn't look surprised at her outburst. "Oh, I'm not going to be texting or calling you anymore. You made sure of that." He walked toward her, and she backed up more. "I just wanted to clear the air between us. You've accused me of some nasty stuff, but I just found out that you were on a date last night."

Ava's mouth dropped open. *How?* She folded her arms. She wasn't able to back up any more since another piano was behind her. "First of all, it wasn't a date. Second of all, we're over so it's not your business."

"Sure, whatever, Ava," Brady said. "You're a hypocrite, and well, no one in the music department is going to be taking your side once they learn the truth."

"My side?" Ava was furious now. "It's not like we were married and our friends have to choose which divorcée they're going to stay friends with. Plus, no one cares if we date or not. Everyone is busy with their own lives, Brady. I know you think the world revolves around you because your granddaddy was one of the university founders, but it really doesn't. You're talented just like the rest of us, and you probably would have gotten in without any connections. You don't have to be a jerk about everything. I know what I saw—and that was when we were dating. Me hanging out with Lane last night is none of your business because we were already broken up."

"He has a name, does he? Lane who?"

Ava was so done with this conversation. She was about to shove past Brady when a man's voice answered from the doorway. "Lane Prosper. Who's asking?"

Ava snapped her gaze to the doorway. There, the man himself stood. Tall. Blond. Cowboy hat and all.

Chapter 11

LANE DIDN'T KNOW IF HE should interrupt, because it seemed like Ava had things well handled. It was good, though, to see that she wasn't pining after Brady in any way, shape, or form. So did that mean she'd officially moved on? That Lane *hadn't* been a rebound? Something that he'd wondered more than once as he turned his truck around and drove all the way back to campus.

Apparently, he'd just taken an eight-hour joyride today.

Not until this moment was he assured it might have been worth it. Ava's face totally transformed. Her eyes lit up, and that smile was back. Everything about her radiated joy. Or was it relief? All mixed with surprise, of course.

"Lane, you—you're here! I thought you'd left this morning."

It was like Brady's head was on a swivel, moving from Ava to Lane, to Ava again.

"I did leave this morning." Lane had no problem holding Brady's gaze and returning whatever glares were thrown at him.

"Are you serious, Ava? *This* guy? He's a little rough around the edges, don't you think?"

"Go away, Brady," Ava shot out. "Leave. Now."

Brady took another look at Lane, then shook his head. "Whatever." He moved away from Ava and strode toward the door. Right at Lane.

He moved out of the doorway, and Brady burst past him. Then the guy had the gall to stop in the doorway and say, "Oh, and good luck. Piano rarely beats violin."

Ava's face flushed, and Lane wondered why. He had figured Brady had entered anyway. Except . . . now he remembered that Ava had said Brady was on full scholarship. So it really was a cheap shot.

"You'll blow him away," Lane said.

Ava was staring at him, and Lane saw the worry there. "He's the best at the school."

Lane walked slowly toward her. "Doesn't matter who's the best. You just gotta connect on an emotional level with the judges."

Ava exhaled. She was all dolled up. Fancy dress, hair up, makeup.

Lane liked her more natural look, but he didn't mind her fancy, either.

"What are you doing here, Lane?" she asked in a quiet voice.

"Wanted to see you perform."

Her face flushed again, but this time, he hoped it was for a different reason, and that she was pleased to see him.

She set a hand on her hip. "So you stuck around for another day? Isn't your family expecting you home?"

"They are. But this felt more important."

A small smile appeared. It was a good thing to see.

"Are you flirting with me, Lane Prosper?"

He was only a couple of feet away from her now. "Maybe a little."

Her smile grew. "Well, thanks for coming to my concert. Even if I don't win, I appreciate the support."

Lane wasn't sure who moved closer, but suddenly, they were only a foot apart. His fingers brushed hers, and her fingers curled around his.

"I didn't sleep much, Ava," he confessed. "Had a lot on my mind."

"Like what?" Her brown eyes sparkled.

He moved his thumb over her hand. "*You.* But I thought the farther away I got from campus, the more I'd forget."

She seemed to inch closer. "And it didn't work?"

"No, ma'am."

Ava smirked. "How far did you get?"

"Four hours."

Her brows popped up. "You just drove *eight* hours?"

"Yep."

Her brow furrowed, though, as if she wasn't impressed in the least. "You mean, it took you four hours of driving to change your mind about coming to my concert?"

Lane chuckled. "Is that what you're worried about?"

She grinned. "Well, however many hours you took, thanks for coming."

They were both grinning now, and Lane wondered if it would be too forward or too presumptuous to kiss her. They had a little bit of privacy, and well, he'd been thinking quite a bit about their kiss last night.

"Oh, there you are," someone said behind them. "I was about to warn you that I saw Brady . . ." The woman's voice trailed off.

Both Lane and Ava turned, releasing hands.

A young woman in a very red dress that was also very fitted, yet was more class than trash, was staring at them, open mouthed. "Ohhh. Sorry. I didn't know you were—"

"Jenni, this is Lane. Lane, this is Jenni."

Jenni gave a feeble wave. Her face was nearly as red as her dress.

"Nice to meet you, Jenni." He touched the brim of his hat.

"Did you just tip your hat to me?" Jenni blurted out. Her gaze shot to Ava. "He just tipped his hat to me. He's like a real cowboy, isn't he?"

Lane wasn't sure if he should be offended, but then Ava laughed. "You can stop drooling now, Jenni. I told you about the hat and boots."

"Am I missing something, ladies?" Lane asked, frowning.

Jenni brought a hand to her chest. "So formal. So polite. Do you have a brother? Unmarried, of course."

Ah. Lane chuckled. "I have two brothers."

"One's married and the other's a bull-rider," Ava said, laughter in her tone.

Jenni blinked. "Well. A bull-rider, huh? Maybe . . ."

"He's attached. Fiancée." Lane looked down at Ava. "What are we doing here? Am I like a matchmaker or something?"

Ava nudged him. "No, you're just hot stuff, and my roommate is feeling left out."

He smirked. "Now it's all making sense."

Her smile was beautiful.

"Okaaay, then, guys," Jenni said with a sigh. "It's pretty dang hot in here, and I need to get some air. Ava, seems like you don't need my warning about you-know-who because you're well taken care of."

"Thanks, Jenni," Ava said. "I would have told you Lane was here, but he surprised me, too."

Jenni released another sigh.

"Besides," Ava continued, "Brady and I already had words. I'm pretty sure he's not going to ever talk to me again. Oh, and he told me that violin always beats piano."

Jenni's eyes went wide. "Wow. Are you serious?"

Ava nodded. "Yes."

Jenni hurried to Ava's side. "Then you'll just have to kick his butt. Show him, and the entire world, who's better."

"Will do." Ava hugged her friend.

But Lane heard the uncertainty in Ava's voice. He wished that this idiot Brady didn't have any power over her self-confidence. Lane just hoped the judges would see through to the heart of the performer as well.

"Okay, bye," Jenni said, releasing Ava. "Nice to meet you, cowboy. I mean, Lane." She was blushing again.

"Nice to meet you, too, Jenni."

"Oh, that accent." Jenni fluttered her hands. "Gotta go. Don't want my seat stolen."

After Jenni had left in a flurry of more goodbyes, Lane looked over at Ava.

She seemed much happier, much more relaxed.

The holding-hands moment was gone, though, especially when another student came in and sat down to warm up with scales. Lane shoved his hands into his pockets. "When do you have to be backstage?"

Ava glanced at the clock on the wall. "About thirty minutes, but I'm done warming up." She motioned toward the other student. "Hard to play at the same time."

"Yeah... So there's no time to grab a coffee or anything?"

"Not really. We can hang out in the hallway, though."

"Sure. Sounds great."

Ava smiled, and they walked out together. She led him to an empty bench outside the practice room.

They sat down, and Ava leaned her head against the wall, but turned her face toward him. "I can't believe you're here. I mean, I'm feeling kind of flattered right now. But the pressure—wow."

"The pressure?"

"You know, I have to win now—with Lane Prosper changing his plans and driving eight hours."

"No pressure. Pretend I'm not even here. Or what is it—pretend the audience is naked?"

"Funny." Ava gave him a quick smile then clasped her hands on her lap. "I mean, that visual would make me more uncomfortable."

He noticed her hands were clasped pretty tightly, and all teasing aside, he wondered if coming back *had* made her more nervous. "Do you mind?" he asked, taking one of her hands and threading their fingers.

"I don't mind."

His heart skipped a couple of beats. Her fingers were cool, but they'd warm up quick, because he felt like he was burning up. "You look beautiful in that dress, Ava. Well, you look beautiful in anything."

Her smile was soft. "As if you've seen a lot of my outfits. Thanks, though. Sometimes I have a hard time with compliments."

Lane squeezed her hand. "You don't say?"

She laughed. "What about you? I'll bet you get them all the time from the ladies. Jenni about had a heart attack."

"Uh, no." Lane shrugged. "I think the reaction to me is more like Brady's . . . you know, the hick thing."

"Hmm." Ava's gaze lingered on him, and well, his lingered on her, too. "How's your family? Your brother and the new baby? Was it born?"

"Oh yeah." Lane released her hand and pulled his phone out of his pocket. "Lucas is the kid's name. Macie's doing fine."

"Oh, wow, so tiny." Ava leaned closer to peer at the picture.

Lane liked her this close. She'd put on perfume, yet it was very subtle.

A text came through—from Knox. It was plain on the screen. *I want details about this woman of yours.*

"Looks like you're in demand."

"Uh . . ." Lane opened the text. There was no hiding it anyway. Ava had already seen it. "I texted Holt that I was heading back to watch your competition. Then I called my mom to tell her. I guess the news spread through the family."

"Your *woman*, huh?" she teased. "What exactly did you tell them? Is there something I should know?"

Lane laughed, but now it was his turn to be nervous. "My family is a bit dramatic—takes things to the extreme."

Ava didn't seem annoyed, so that was a good sign, right? Because Lane's pulse was jumping all over the place right now. He really liked this girl . . . but things were kind of impossible between them. So why was he here? Adding more time and memories between them for him to dwell on later?

He replied to Knox. *Chill, bro. There's nothing to tell except that I'm delaying my return to attend a concert.* He glanced at Ava, who wasn't making any secret of watching him texting. *If there's something more, I'm sure you'll find out through Mom.*

Knox's reply came back immediately. *I'll hold you to that, bro.*

Lane put his phone on silent, then pocketed it, because he didn't really trust what Knox might text him next.

"Sorry about that," Lane said. "I swear I'm not stalking you or anything. I just . . . well, I don't really know. I'm here and I guess I'm sort of wondering if it was the right thing or not. Because now my entire family seems to be involved."

He took a breath and waited for Ava to reply. To give him some slack.

She said nothing, though. Instead, *she* reached for his hand this time.

Well, that was completely fine with him.

Chapter 12

Ava was swooning, hard.

Was this what crushing meant? She'd liked guys before—but this was different. She was older, more mature, had been in relationships, and Lane Prosper was a full-grown man. The cowboy side only added to that, and it didn't hurt that he had graduated with goals and aspirations.

He was also solid, down to earth, and looked at her like she was his favorite dessert.

Butterflies had been zooming in her stomach ever since he'd walked into the practice room, and now, he was sitting in the front row of the auditorium with Jenni.

Ava could see the pair of them through the opening in the partition separating the main stage from the back area where contestants waited, sitting or pacing before their names were called. Brady was hanging out with another violinist—Bethany—and they looked cozy. Already. Yeah, there was a pit in Ava's stomach, but not because Brady was openly flirting. Because she'd been so gullible.

No more, she decided. She refocused her attention through the narrow opening and saw Jenni say something to

Lane, who nodded in agreement. She half-wished she were sitting with the pair of them instead of getting ready to perform.

Ava released a sigh. A swoony sigh. Lane had driven eight hours to come to her concert. This meant last night hadn't been a fluke. This meant Lane felt things—maybe the same things she'd felt. This meant she hadn't been rebounding after Brady. She wasn't confused. She wasn't bitter. She was . . . moving forward. Moving on.

What would happen with Lane, though?

Just because he was here tonight didn't mean he'd be here tomorrow or the next day. He'd be leaving at some point. Probably soon.

"Did you see the lineup?" Georgia asked, approaching Ava with a program.

She had, but she took it anyway. "Thanks." She'd be the last to perform. Torture, to say the least. Brady was listed somewhere in the middle.

The Dean of Music finished his announcements and introduced the judges. Then the audience broke out into applause as Jorge walked onto the stage, carrying his cello. He took a seat, then began his number.

It would be a good hour before Ava's turn, and she didn't know if time was passing too fast or too slow. Georgia did her piano number, then Bethany on the violin. Next up was Brady. His violin performance was stellar, and the audience clapped enthusiastically. The judges had looked impressed, too—Ava had peeked through the partition. She'd have to outshine him by quite a bit to get the judges' attention. Lane's words moved through her mind—he wanted her to play her unpolished piece.

Finally, it was her turn, and Ava kept her mind perfectly blank as she walked out onto the stage. The clapping was polite, but she could swear she heard Lane's and Jenni's above the rest. Instead of taking a seat at the piano, she stepped up to the microphone. "I've changed the number I'll be performing."

No one in the audience would care—well, almost no one. She could feel Lane's gaze upon her as she moved to the piano. How, she couldn't exactly explain it.

She knew the piece was rough, but maybe, like Lane had said, she could get by with it. When she'd played it with Lane as the sole audience, she'd been upset with Brady. Well, she was still upset with him, truth be told, but she was mostly upset at herself. A new beginning was on the horizon for her—without Lane, of course, but spending time with him had taught her how she'd put too much of her self-worth into Brady.

She shouldn't do that with any person.

Her fingers moved over the keys, but her nerves were interfering.

Focus on the notes, she told herself.

No, focus on the feeling.

There. Her fingers were more agile now, and she glossed over an error, racing up the keyboard, then back down.

She felt it now. Transported. She was only a vehicle for the music. It flowed through her, not from her. She didn't even realize how close she was to the end until the final stanzas began. Slowing down, she took more time than usual, singling out the treble-clef notes and muting the bass chords.

The final notes wove together, and the sound faded until it was completely gone.

Only then did Ava realize she had tears in her eyes. And only then did she lift her hands from the keys.

There was no sound from the audience.

Not one person was clapping.

Maybe she'd messed up more than she'd realized.

She rose to her feet, her knees unsteady, and turned to face the audience.

Just before she bowed, several people leapt to their feet and started clapping.

Others stood, clapping, too.

Within a few heartbeats, the entire audience was on their feet, clapping as if Ava had done something stunning.

She drew in a trembling breath and bowed. When she straightened, she dared a glance at Lane and Jenni.

They were both on their feet, grinning and clapping.

Ava knew she should leave the stage, but her feet remained rooted as the thunderous clapping continued. She'd put on the performance of her life.

It seemed to go on forever, but was probably only a minute or two. When she made it off the stage, she wanted to collapse in a heap. Her heart was pounding so hard that she could barely catch her breath.

Several of the students congratulated her. Others only nodded. A few ignored her.

She didn't care. Whatever the outcome, whomever the winner was, she'd pushed herself harder than she ever had before. That was something to be proud of.

The Dean of Music announced into the microphone that the judges had their decision and asked all the performers to come onto the stage.

With watery legs, Ava headed there. Everyone stood in a line. The waiting felt like torture, and her heart felt like it was about to take flight.

One of the judges stood up, and rambled about how talented everyone was.

Ava had a hard time focusing on what he said, and the stage lights seemed much too bright now. Had they been that way when she was playing?

"And our winner for this year's contest is . . . Bethany Jensen."

The audience was so silent that Ava was sure everyone could hear her thundering heartbeat.

Bethany. The winner is Bethany.

The clapping started, but it was half-hearted—or was Ava just imagining that?

Bethany had done a great job, hadn't she? Ava wasn't sure. She hadn't really paid attention to Bethany's violin piece.

The judge walked toward the grinning Bethany and handed over a golden trophy, along with a large envelope. Probably the check for the contest money.

It's fine, Ava told herself. *At least Brady didn't win . . .*

Brady stepped up and hugged Bethany, congratulating her. Others crowded around to congratulate Bethany, too. Ava should go over to her. It was just a contest. Someone had to win, and it was a long shot that she would.

Brady and Bethany were sure cozy . . .

Ava didn't care if they became a couple, she really didn't, but right now—this was all a lot to take in. She crossed to Bethany. "Congratulations, I'm so happy for you."

And she was, but she felt like a boulder was sitting on her chest. She needed to get away from the crowd and the conversations and just go somewhere quiet to breathe . . .

Ava headed backstage, then paused to look to where Jenni and Lane sat. They had already left, and Ava assumed she'd meet up with them later. At least she hoped so with Lane. Her thoughts had scattered everywhere, and she barely acknowledged those who spoke to her as she headed to the back door of the auditorium.

In the hallway, she scanned for Lane and Jenni, but Ava didn't see them right away. She sent Jenni a text that she'd be walking home. Then she texted Lane, too.

A walk in the warm night would do her good.

Clear her head.

The tears came, and Ava wiped them away. She'd pinned too much on this contest. It was okay to feel let down, but the blow felt bigger because Lane had come back to watch her. And maybe because Bethany's win had been unexpected. Brady's wouldn't have surprised her, though.

Ava called her mom, and she answered on the first ring. After spilling all that had happened, her mom said, "You can't change the past, honey. For some reason, you lost unfairly, but maybe that's because there are better things in store for your future."

Ava couldn't imagine what that could be. "How are you feeling?"

"A little better. I just need a solid night's sleep. I was waiting to take my cough medicine until after you called."

"Take it, Mom, I'll be fine. I'll just keep putting one foot in front of the other."

"That's my girl."

By the time Ava reached her apartment, her tears had dried, but her heart still felt bruised.

She slowed when she saw Lane's truck. He and Jenni were standing near the door.

"Oh, there you are," Jenni said. "We almost sent out a search party."

"No need," Ava said, hating that her voice trembled. "I'm here."

"I'm so sorry." Jenni stepped forward and hugged her.

That only started the tears all over again, but Ava appreciated her friend. "Thanks. Bethany was great, and well, I did my best. So whatever."

Jenni pulled away. "You don't get it, do you?"

"Get what?"

"*You* were the best. The audience reaction proved that. The judges were blown away." Jenni bit her lip and glanced over at Lane. "We think it was rigged."

Ava scoffed. "No, those things aren't rigged. The judges are all . . ." She thought about it—they were all music professors. "What are you saying, Jenni?"

"I don't have proof, of course," Jenni said. "But Brady and Bethany were really cozy. And it was weird that he entered in the first place. Maybe to prove that not the best musician would win—him—and so then you couldn't complain about not winning, either."

Ava didn't move for a moment, then she shook her head. "Bethany won, and that's how it goes. It's fine. Really. I'm just sad about the money." She laughed, but it sounded hollow, even to her.

"Bethany was fine, just not amazing like you were," Jenni said. "But I'm starving, and I'm going to order some food for all of us. See you upstairs."

Jenni took off, leaving Ava to face Lane.

"Sorry you came back to see me lose," she ventured, hoping she sounded like she was teasing, when inside, she still felt raw.

"You didn't lose in my book," Lane said, the edges of his mouth lifting. "You showed that piano who's boss."

"You bet I did."

"Come here." Lane stepped toward her and opened his arms.

She stepped into them. Everything between them had been light and flirty, but this hug was more intimate . . . more personal. Comforting. Secure. His arms were steady, his heartbeat strong, and he smelled of cotton and warm sun.

"You're going to make me cry again," she said, feeling her eyes burn.

He moved one of his hands along her back, and she nestled closer. How had this man so quickly become like a rock to her?

She drew away then, because all kinds of feelings were running through her, and he'd be heading to Texas once and for all soon . . .

"Well, thanks for coming all this way, Lane," she said, looking up at him. His face was shadowed by his hat beneath the streetlamp, but she felt the warmth of his gaze regardless. "You coming up? The least we could do is feed you. And if you need a place to crash, our couch is decent."

Where *was* he planning on sleeping? His truck? A hotel? Back at his empty place?

"Well, I won't turn down food, but I don't want to impose on your place. Even if it is the couch."

Ava reached for his hand. "Well, we can decide that later. Let's go find out what kind of damage Jenni did."

Lane squeezed her hand, and she squeezed back. They began walking toward the apartment building, and Lane asked, "You okay, Ava?"

"Yeah."

He nodded. "You were amazing. Not that you don't always play amazing, but in an auditorium filled with people, it was just that much more powerful."

"Thanks," she said. "It felt amazing."

He grabbed the door and opened it, then they headed inside.

She led him up the flight of stairs to the apartment. Jenni had some music playing and was doing the dishes.

"Ah-ha, you caught me," she said with a laugh.

"Wow, first time you've done dishes in like a month," Ava teased. Her bruised heart felt better now, and she was pretty sure it was because Lane was by her side.

"Trying to impress your cowboy," Jenni quipped.

Ava turned to Lane. "Ignore everything Jenni says."

"Hey," Jenni said.

"Want a water bottle or soda?" Ava asked, opening the fridge door.

"Water's fine," Lane said.

She handed him a cold water bottle. "Have a seat. Your choices are one of the rickety kitchen chairs, that bean bag, or our very comfy couch."

Lane seemed to take this into serious consideration, then opted for the couch.

Ava tried not to dwell on the fact that Lane Prosper was here, in her apartment, sitting on her couch, his cowboy hat on their side table. Because he'd driven back to watch her perform.

It was better to distract herself. "What did you order, Jenni?"

"Pizza from Ricardo's."

"How am I not surprised?" she teased, then looked over at Lane. "Jenni has pizza like five times a week."

"Well, you do, too," Jenni said.

"That's because you order it, and I'm just helping you out by eating it."

"Hey, I like pizza, too," Lane said.

Jenni beamed at him. "The best thing about it is I can call up and ask for my usual order. Although this time I doubled it for you."

"Ah, thank you," Lane said. "What's your Venmo? I'll send you some money."

Jenni waved a hand. "Oh, it's fine. It's my treat. I'm not as broke as Ava, you know."

"He knows." Ava sat on the opposite side of the couch from Lane. Maybe she'd been too open with him, but it was too late now. He'd known how much she was hoping to win the competition tonight to get tuition paid for. "Wish me luck getting a job that will stick for the summer. No one's going to hire me full-time temporarily, so I'll be working two part-time jobs."

Jenni sat cross-legged on the beanbag. "You'll find something, Ava, you always do."

Ava could only hope, though it would mean working all hours, and not having a break to maybe visit a handsome cowboy in Texas. If he'd even want that. But he was here, wasn't he? He looked fairly comfortable on her couch, and those eyes of his were on her again. Expectant.

Chapter 13

LANE HAD JUST THOUGHT OF the most crazy idea ever. Well, maybe it wasn't crazy. No, it definitely was. But the more he listened to Jenni and Ava talk about jobs, classes, and renewing their dorm apartment lease, the more he wondered if Ava would go for his idea . . .

The doorbell rang.

"Pizza's here." Jenni jumped up from the beanbag and hurried to the door. She thanked the pizza delivery guy profusely, which made Lane chuckle. She really did like her pizza.

Ava dragged the coffee table over between the couch and bean bag. Then Jenni turned on the TV to some comedy station.

The pizza was good, Lane decided, really good. And it was nice to have Ava laughing at the comedy skit with her friend. She seemed to have moved past the loss from tonight, but still, he wondered.

They ate and laughed, and Jenni told stories about Ava that were hilarious. Then Ava dug right back at her roommate and told her own stories. All the while, Lane kept wondering. But it wasn't something he wanted to ask with Jenni around.

So he had to wait. He'd finally accepted their offer to crash on their couch. He didn't really have another place lined up anyway. At one point, he went through his multiple text messages. There were more pictures of baby Lucas. His mom had texted to ask what his new traveling plans were. Knox had texted to see how the concert went, and Evie had texted the same thing.

Nothing from Cara, but with her being in California, she wasn't always up-to-date on the family drama and/or shenanigans.

"Well, good night, everyone," Jenni said. "See y'all in the morning. See what I did there?"

Lane smiled. "I see. Good night, Miss Jenni."

"Ah, that drawl. It's killing me!" She headed down the hall.

Finally, it was just Lane and Ava. The TV was still on, but turned low, so it was impossible to follow whatever was on. The pizza and drinks had long been cleaned up.

"So . . ." Ava said, pulling her legs up on the couch and facing him. "Heading out in the morning? Is that your new plan?"

"I think so," Lane said. "I'm not in any rush, though, not anymore."

Ava smiled. "Well, you do need to drive safe."

He nodded. He was glad he'd come back—to see her in person, to hear her voice, to watch her perform, to hold her hand, to count her freckles . . .

Silence fell between them, and there was really no reason to put this off any longer. The idea would not leave his head, which meant he'd better share it. Plus, it was after midnight, and she was probably tired . . .

"So, uh, I had a question—an idea, actually."

Ava's brows lifted. "Oh really? What's that?"

Take a Chance

Lane paused, his heart thumping. He was really going to do this—ask her. "Since you didn't win tonight, and you're in between things—without a job and such..."

She smirked. "True."

"I thought maybe you could take a little break, you know, get away for a bit. Clear your head. The grind will always be here, waiting for you to jump in." He exhaled. He was doing a poor job of explaining. "How about you come to Prosper with me, for a week or two? Just to hang out. Then, when you've had enough, I'll put you on a plane back here."

Ava blinked. "What?"

"I know it sounds kind of impulsive, but maybe it's not, maybe it's—" He broke off. "Look, I like you, Ava, and for whatever reason, we didn't meet until yesterday. I just don't like the idea of me leaving in the morning and never seeing you again."

"We really don't know each other," Ava said, but her tone wasn't wary, it was... warm.

"We can remedy some of that on a long road trip."

The edges of her mouth curved. "I think you're sweet, Lane Prosper, I do. But heading off to Texas with you is kind of a big deal."

"Only if you think of it as a big deal," he said, turning more fully toward her on the couch. "It's more of a break. Something fun and distracting. Heck, most of my family will be around. You could stay in Cara's room. And if you think it's all too weird after a day or two, then just say the word, and you'll be on a plane."

Ava looked down at her clasped hands. They were gripped tight. "It sounds..."

When she didn't finish, Lane said, "Terrible?"

She lifted her head, and her brown eyes seemed to be golden with warmth. "Amazing, actually." She laughed. "I can't believe you'd want to take me to Prosper with you."

Heat flashed through Lane's chest. "I don't think it should be too much of a surprise. I mean, you are a pretty amazing human."

Ava nudged his knee with her foot. "You're laying it on thick, sir."

He reached for her hand and slid his fingers through hers. "So, is that a yes?"

She looked down at their interlocked hands, then back up at him. "Yes."

He tugged her hand toward him, and she unfolded her legs, then scooted close.

Lane slipped his arm around her shoulders, then grasped her other hand. She could probably hear his heart pounding something fierce.

Ava leaned into him, her head nestled beneath his chin. "Just because I'm coming to Prosper with you doesn't mean I want things between us to, um, move fast. We're going as friends, you know."

"Oh, I absolutely agree."

She lifted her head at this, turned, and peered at him. "You do?"

"Yes, ma'am." He held her gaze. "I don't want you to break my heart."

Ava's mouth quirked.

He was tempted to kiss her then, but he held back. Friends didn't kiss, did they?

"You really think *I* could break your heart, Lane Prosper? I'm pretty sure if we were dating, which we aren't, but *if* we were, then the women would be lined up to distract you when we broke up. Jenni would probably be in that line, too."

"But none of them would be you." Lane released her hand to run a thumb along her jaw. She was so close, so kissable, but if she really wanted to be friends, then he'd honor that. Maybe it would change. Hopefully it would change.

Her breath caught, and Lane wondered what was going through her mind.

He moved his hand along her neck, then over her shoulder, and down her arm. When his hand linked with hers again, she leaned close, pressing against him, and kissed his cheek. "Thanks for understanding about the friendship thing, Lane. What time do you want to leave?"

His mind was spinning too much to comprehend her question. "Uh . . ."

"Early? I need an hour to get ready, so whatever time works for you works for me."

"Eight is fine. I mean, we gotta get some sleep."

She pulled away and stood.

He wanted to pull her back. Fine, they wouldn't kiss, but they could still hold hands. Right?

"I'll bring you a blanket and pillow, then see you in the morning."

And she did just that, for better or for worse. Lane lay awake at least another hour, his mind arguing against his idea. But in the end, Ava had accepted, and tomorrow, he'd be taking a woman home to meet his family.

And he was completely fine with it, even if Ava had insisted on staying friends. It was a wise decision, after all. His family would be all over them if they thought they were dating, or anything serious. This way, Ava could have her break, and Lane could spend more time with her before moving to North Carolina. Not that he'd decided to take the job, but it was there, and it would be a good opportunity. He just wanted to . . . figure everything out in his head. About Ava. He only hoped he'd have an answer before the deadline in a week.

The morning came faster than Lane thought it would, which meant he'd gotten some decent sleep. He rummaged in the kitchen and had some eggs cooking by the time Ava came down the hallway.

"Good morning." He grinned at the sight of her. Her hair was pulled back into a loose ponytail, and she wore a ratty T-shirt with cut-off sweats that he guessed doubled as sleeping shorts? No makeup or fancy stuff. Lane liked it that way.

"I guess you're a morning person?" Ava said, her voice a rasp.

"Yes, ma'am."

"It's too early for *ma'am*."

He only chuckled and caught her hand before she could move past him to the fridge. "Still coming to Texas?"

She turned toward him, her brown eyes bright in the morning sun coming through the front room. "I am. Unless you changed your mind?"

He shifted closer. "Nope."

Ava blinked up at him. "You need to stop that."

"Stop what?"

"Being so . . . you know. Hot stuff."

"Did you change your mind?"

"About coming? No."

"About us staying only friends?"

"No again." She patted his chest, then pushed him back. "That smells really good. Might even wake Jenni from the dead. She sleeps through everything." Ava opened the fridge and pulled out a half-gallon of orange juice.

"Hope I wasn't imposing going through your kitchen."

"Oh, heavens no," Jenni blurted as she walked in. "Wow, Ava. Where did you find this man?" She moved past the both of them and poured herself a glass of orange juice, then turned with a smirk. She was also dressed in something resembling pajamas—a giant T-shirt with a cartoon figure on the front.

"Good morning, Jenni," Lane said.

"Good morning, Lane," she said back, then her gaze moved to Ava. "What did I miss? You're staying friends? Because he's leaving today?"

"Sort of—I mean, I'm going to Texas with him for a week," Ava said in a rush, as if she were nervous. "And well, it's just for a short break, then I'll be back. So it's better we, um, stay friends and all that."

Jenni had paused with the orange juice halfway to her mouth. She set it down. "Wait. What? You're leaving me?"

"You're welcome to come, too, Jenni," Lane offered.

"No," Ava said at the same time Jenni said, "Really?"

"I mean," Ava said, trying to recover, "you should come."

Lane loved that Ava was clearly *not* wanting her friend along. Maybe that meant she was looking forward to their time together as much as he was.

"Oh, dang," Jenni said in a semi-fake voice. "I have that thing tomorrow, and that other thing the next day."

Ava's brows shot up. "I'm serious, Jenni. Come with us."

Jenni picked up her orange juice. "Can't." Then she took a sip and walked out of the kitchen, calling out, "I want a hug before you leave. From both of you!"

Her bedroom door shut, and Ava released a sigh. "I think she's mad."

"I think she'll get over it," Lane said.

Ava shifted her gaze to him. "What are you smiling about?"

"You're a nice friend, but I'm glad you didn't truly want her on our road trip."

Ava's cheeks pinked. "I just think it would be less . . . complicated. And well, we can get to know each other easier without my swooning best friend along."

"I have no complaints. So we're back to Plan A?"

Ava's smile was slow. "Yes, sir. I need to call my mom and let her know what's going on, but otherwise Plan A is still on."

Lane was more than excited that Ava was going to be coming with him, but it was going to be hard staying in the friend zone.

Chapter 14

AVA'S FIRST IMPRESSION OF THE town of Prosper was that the dark sky seemed to be miles long, with millions of glittering stars overhead. The past thirteen hours of driving had been remarkable and fascinating, talking to Lane Prosper. Nothing really fazed him, not even the dynamics of his large family.

She'd always wanted a sibling, but hadn't realized how involved a large family was. With five siblings in the Prosper family and two grandkids, plus a daughter-in-law and some significant others, Lane's phone never seemed to stop.

"How do you get anything done?" Ava had teased him.

"Oh, it's just the weekend. Everyone's abuzz with the birth of Lucas, too." Lane had squeezed her hand.

So, yeah, they'd held hands a lot on the drive. But no other type of snuggling had taken place, and definitely no kissing. Ava was holding firm to the friend zone with Lane because, well, everything seemed too good to be true.

She was glad she'd agreed to come along, because she was very intrigued by Lane. It seemed the feeling was mutual, and Ava would analyze that later.

But overall, spending a week with Lane—and his family—would dunk her headfirst into who he was at the core.

There was no better way to get to know a person, Ava guessed. So that's what she was doing.

Besides, a week away from the university and job hunting wouldn't change the fact that she was broke. She could fill out job applications online, and maybe even do some interviews over the phone.

Lane had assured her it would all work out.

And she'd decided to believe him.

They'd been driving along a small country road for what felt like forever, but maybe that was because Ava was anxious now.

She'd be meeting Lane's parents and his sister Evie soon.

Ava told herself not to be intimidated because there were no expectations anywhere.

Another text buzzed Lane's phone.

Lane glanced at the incoming message. "Tell her five minutes."

Ava picked up his phone. She'd been playing his secretary most of the drive. After texting Lane's mom, Ava leaned forward. "Those trees are amazing."

The road was literally tree-lined for what seemed like a mile, and the moon peeked through the branches, making everything look like a storybook.

"You should see them in the daylight."

Ava peered at Lane. "I think you secretly love this place."

"Oh, I love it," Lane said, slowing his truck down as he followed a curve. "I just don't want to live here the rest of my life. It's so small-town."

"Got it." She squeezed his hand, and he squeezed back.

She loved his larger hand encasing her smaller one.

"So . . . if we're going to be just friends," his voice rumbled as his thumb moved over her fingers, "I guess I can't be holding your hand around people?"

She ignored the goosebumps racing up her arm. "Probably best."

"Let me know if you change your mind."

Ava furrowed her brow. "Why? You said you agreed."

"That was last night." He brought her hand to his lips and pressed a soft kiss there. "Before I got to know you better."

Lane Prosper certainly knew how to charm her, but Ava was going to stick to her word. Yeah, she'd rambled about all kinds of stories. Growing up stuff with her mom, high school stuff, college stuff. She couldn't believe how talkative she'd been around him. With Brady, she hadn't shared nearly so much in the months they'd dated. It seemed like their conversations had always been centered around *his* stories and *his* experiences.

"Well, friends is the best I can do right now, under these circumstances," she said. "As of today, we live in two different states."

Lane lowered her hand. "I guess you're right. But what if the circumstances were different?" he teased.

Or at least she thought he was teasing.

Ava cracked a smile. "They're not different. And, oh, is that your house?"

Lane shifted his gaze back to the road. "Sure is."

The ranch house was a sprawling white rambler. "It's really beautiful. A wraparound porch is to die for. And all of this property—I can't even imagine. No one would see each other for days."

"Oh, trust me, you'll see plenty of people." Lane slowed the truck and parked next to another one that looked dusty but a lot newer.

As if on cue, the front door opened, and light spilled onto the porch in a bright yellow rectangle. Two people emerged. No, three.

One was a smaller person.

"Uncle Lane!" the little girl hollered as soon as Lane had cut the engine and popped open his door. "Grandpa said I could stay up until you got here!"

Lane hopped out of the truck, and before Ava could get her bearings and reach for the door handle, he'd opened her door. He held her hand while he helped her down, then let go of it.

"How was the drive, son?" the older woman asked.

"Just fine," Lane said. "Bit stiff is all, but the truck ran great. This is Ava Sampson, everyone. Ava, this is my mom Heidi and my dad Rex."

Heidi was blonde like her son, but Ava suspected it was from a bottle in her case. Her hair was cut into a no-nonsense bob, and she wore carefully applied makeup. Rex seemed dressed for company, wearing a pressed button-down blue shirt and tan Levi's. His large belt buckle read "Prosperity Ranch."

"What about me?" the little girl asked. Her brown eyes were huge, and her brown curls bounced when she talked.

"Oh, and Ruby is around here somewhere. Has anyone seen her?" Lane pretended to look for her.

"I'm down here, silly."

"Oh, there you are." He scooped her up and swung her around, making her giggle. He leaned toward his mother and kissed her cheek, then gave his dad a half-hug.

"Glad y'all made it safely." Heidi's warm smile landed on Ava. "And nice to meet your girl."

"Nice to meet you, too." Ava stuck out her hand, wondering if she should correct the "your girl" phrase.

"Oh, we hug in this family," Lane's mom said, pulling Ava into a tight hug.

Surprised, Ava hugged her back.

"Welcome to Prosperity Ranch," his dad said, giving her a light hug as well.

"Ava's a pretty name," Ruby announced.

Ava smiled. "Ruby's a pretty name, too."

Ruby grinned and turned her brown eyes on her uncle. "I like her, Uncle Lane. Where did you get her?"

Everyone chuckled.

"Do you mean where is she from?" Lane said.

Ruby scrunched her nose. "Yeah, where is she from?"

Lane cut a glance at Ava. "She's from Arizona, where I was in school."

"Oh." Ruby pushed against his chest. "Put me down. I want to show you my baby brother."

"Is he here?" Lane asked.

"No, silly." Ruby wriggled out of Lane's arms and opened the door with two hands. "He's on Grandpa's phone. They're just pictures."

Lane chuckled.

"Hang on, sweet pea," Rex said. "Grandpa needs to find his phone first."

Heidi smiled after her husband and granddaughter, then she looked at Lane and Ava. "Do you need help unloading?"

"I got it, Mom," Lane said. "I'll just grab what we need tonight and unload the rest in the morning. You can show Ava around."

"Well, come in, then. Did Lane tell you that you'll be in Cara's old room?"

"He did," Ava said.

Lane brushed against her as he turned and headed back to the truck. She kind of wanted to stay outside with him and help unload their bags. Or maybe it was to spend a little more alone time with Lane before stepping into the family house. She was already missing their time together—which was strange, because they were still together.

Just with people around, like Lane had warned her.

"Right through here," his mom said, holding the door open.

Ava stepped into the cozy ranch house. The front room had a plaid-patterned couch and love seat and oak furnishings. An upright piano was stuffed in the corner of the room. Heidi saw Ava looking at it. "You're welcome to play it anytime. Lane said that you practice several hours a day?"

"At least a couple," Ava said. "Either way, I'm on vacation." She'd never gone more than a day or two without practicing, so maybe she'd get a couple of stints in.

They walked past the kitchen, where Ruby was with Rex at the oak kitchen table. She was busy pointing out which pictures were the best ones to show Lane.

"Kitchen," Heidi said with an affectionate smile toward the pair. "There are basically two sections of bedrooms. One with mine and the boys' old rooms. Then the girls have their own section. We always felt like we needed to keep a close eye on the comings and goings of our sons."

Ava smiled. She knew the comment was lighthearted, but there was definitely some difficult family history the Prospers had lived through. Lane had filled her in on more details about his brother Knox and Macie's quick marriage, then their complicated divorce. How Macie had brought Ruby for the summer to Prosperity Ranch, and that was when she and Holt forged a deep connection.

"Does everyone stay here when they come back to Prosper?"

"Oh, well, not anymore," Heidi said as they walked along the hall. "Evie is living here now, but Knox stays with Jana. Holt has his own house. Cara usually stays at the bed and breakfast. Likes her extra space, I guess."

"Ah. And is Evie home?" Ava didn't mean to pry, but she

also wondered why the sister Lane had been communicating with more than once on the drive wasn't here to meet him like she'd said.

"Oh, she'll be here any minute." Heidi paused before a door and opened it. "She's with her boyfriend, Carson Hunt. He lives just down the road."

Yeah, Ava had been told about Evie's boyfriend—a transplant to Prosper.

"Here's your bedroom."

The room was painted in a pale gray, and the furnishings were all white. The place felt clean and fresh. "It's lovely."

"Well, it's clean," Heidi said with a half-laugh. "Cara would never let me decorate, so even though she's been gone for a few years, I still keep it how she liked it."

A commotion coming from down the hallway—likely the front door—told Ava that the other sister must have showed up.

Heidi opened the closet door. "There's plenty of room here, but if you need more, there's a closet in the hallway, too. Oh, and these old houses don't have bathrooms for every bedroom, so you'll have to share with Evie."

"That's totally fine," Ava said. "I lived in a one-bedroom apartment with my mom for a decade. Anything upgraded from a couch is like heaven to me." She'd meant it to sound funny, but Heidi's brow furrowed.

"Oh, my dear. I'm sorry to hear that. Lane hasn't told us much about you, but I'd love to hear all about your family when we have more time."

The voices in the front part of the house were louder now.

Ava just nodded, because a lump had formed in her throat for some reason.

"I guess we'll go say hi to the others before they track us

down." Heidi walked toward the bedroom door. "Oh, and Ava. I know that Lane said you'd be staying for a week, but you're welcome to stay as long as you want."

"I think a week will be plenty," Ava said. "I don't want to wear out my welcome or intrude on your family."

"Believe me, you're not," Heidi said. "I love company, and well, I love seeing my son with . . . so much light in his eyes."

"Light?" Ava echoed.

"He's too serious, always has been," Heidi said. "But the past two days, in our phone conversations, something has shifted. And I'm pretty sure it has to do with you."

Ava didn't know if she could take credit for anything about Lane, and she didn't want to. They were just friends. "Mrs. Prosper, Lane and I only met a couple of days ago. I don't think that whatever change you've noticed has to do with *me*. He just graduated college, so I'm sure that's a huge load off his mind."

"Maybe," Heidi said with a slight shrug. "We can debate these finer points later. Let's get you introduced to the others."

The minute Ava stepped into the front room, she was swept into a whirlwind of introductions. Evie was definitely Lane's sister.

Ava was surprised she wore a summer dress. Maybe she had thought Evie would be more of a tomboy and wearing jeans and a plaid shirt? Her dark blonde hair was styled in long waves that fell to halfway down her back.

Evie's boyfriend, Carson, had dark, wavy hair and dark eyes—so brown they were nearly black.

"And this is my oldest brother, Holt," Lane said as he introduced her around.

Ava could have guessed that since Holt had the same blue eyes as most of his siblings, although his hair was brown instead of blond. And Ruby was hanging off of him like a baby gorilla.

"Great to finally meet you, Ava," Holt said.

Finally? After only a couple of days? She smiled. "Nice to meet you, too. And congratulations on your new baby."

"Thanks, but it was all Macie's doing." He paused. "Well, mostly."

Everyone laughed.

"Daddy, what's so funny?"

"Uh," Holt said. "Just that parenting is a lot of work?"

"Is that why I have two daddies?" Ruby asked, but before Holt could answer, she looked at Ava. "Did you know I have two daddies?" She held up two small fingers for emphasis. "But baby Lucas only has one. I told him I would share my other daddy with him."

"Ruby," Heidi said. "How about you help me fix a plate of cookies?"

"Okay!" Ruby zoomed on her little feet straight for the kitchen.

"So, was the drive good?" Holt asked, changing the subject completely. "No issues with the old truck?"

"It was great," Lane said, his arm brushing Ava's. "Truck purred the entire way."

She kind of wanted him to hold her hand, but suppressed that quickly.

"Good news, bro," Holt said. "But it's like a ticking timer. Maybe when you get that dream job offer, you can spring for something a little newer than twenty years."

"Maybe."

Lane's tone was light, but Ava knew this was a tired subject between him and his family.

The next hour passed quickly with everyone chatting. Heidi brought out some cookies, but tried to talk them into eating leftover casserole. Ava didn't want to be rude, but bed was sounding like the best thing right now.

Finally, everyone who wasn't staying at the house left, and Lane walked Ava down the hall. Even though she'd enjoyed meeting his family, she was ready to call it a night.

"This is probably as far as I should go." Lane grasped her hand and tugged her to a stop a few feet before the door of the bedroom.

"You're holding my hand."

The edge of his mouth lifted. "I am."

"I'll let it slide this time."

He chuckled. His touch was so warm, solid, and made her pulse jumpy. "So, what did you think of the Prosper clan? I don't think my mom could stop smiling and talking to you."

Ava's neck warmed. "She's a sweetheart, Lane. Your whole family is great. And you're right. There's a lot going on—but in a good way."

"But?" he prompted, his blue eyes scanning her face. "You were more quiet than I thought you'd be."

She shrugged. "The drive with you was nice, you know. Just us. It's weird, but I kind of miss being with just you—even though you're right here."

His brows lifted. "Dang. I wish I could kiss you right now, but that would totally cross the friend-zone line."

Yes, it would. "Good night, Lane." She squeezed his hand then let go. One more minute, or even one more second standing with him in the quiet hallway would probably result in a kiss.

She opened the bedroom door, then turned and gave him a little wave.

He was standing there, alone, his hands in his pockets, his blue eyes endless with warmth.

Chapter 15

Lane paced the porch. He'd been up for three hours, and still no sign of Ava waking up. He'd even told his mom to peek in, but she'd been sound asleep.

Well, she had been through a lot the past couple of days.

Just because the first sounds of morning ranch life kicked into Lane's bloodstream didn't mean that Ava would be the same.

Still... where was she?

"Good morning," his mom murmured from inside the house.

Ava had to be up. No one else was home right now.

Lane strode into the house, taking his hat off, as his mother had always demanded.

Ava stood next to the kitchen counter, holding a glass of juice. She was showered, dressed, and they'd have to do something about those dainty sandals of hers. At least she was wearing jeans—jeans that were well-worn and fit her perfectly.

She'd braided her hair into two braids, and they hung over her shoulders, her dark hair color contrasting with the faded red T-shirt she wore.

Her gaze locked with his as he approached. "Good morning," he said.

Her lips tilted upward. "Good morning."

"Sleep well?" He stopped a couple of feet in front of her.

His mom was in the kitchen, and he probably shouldn't sweep Ava into a tight hug even though he wanted to.

"I did." Her smile appeared. "I just told your mom that I can't remember the last time I slept in so long."

Lane cut a glance at the clock. "It is ten in the morning, but if you're not a morning person . . ."

"I always sign up for early classes, even though I'm not a morning person."

"That's right. You told me on the drive yesterday."

Her eyes danced. Were her memories as good as his? With what she said to him last night right before their *non-kiss* good night, it had been very tough to fall asleep. But she seemed to have no problem sleeping here.

"I told you a lot of things on the drive. Maybe it was too much."

"It wasn't too much," Lane said. "You can tell me anything you want."

His mother cleared her throat.

Lane looked over at her. Her brows were raised, her mouth pressed together to suppress a smile or a laugh. "Good morning, Mom."

"Good morning, son. You've been pacing like a cheetah out there," his mom said. "What's the plan for the day?"

"Oh, are we late for something?" Ava asked.

"No," Lane said quickly. "I was just . . . thinking. Holt and I have a meeting later today to go over finances. But the morning's yours. Whatever you want to do, we'll do it."

His mother gave a soft laugh, then she stood from the kitchen table. "I'll leave you two to work things out. If you need anything, I'll be in the quilting room. Lunch is at noon. Just text me if you make other plans."

"Oh, we'll eat in town," Lane said. "If that's all right, Mom? At some point, I want to stop in and see the baby. If that's all right with you, Ava?"

Both women, at the same time, said, "That's all right."

Ava laughed. His mom smiled and headed out of the room, first stopping to kiss Lane on the cheek, then patting his arm.

Once his mom was out of earshot, Lane turned to Ava. "I wasn't pacing like a cheetah."

She took a sip of her juice, then smirked. "You were sweating bullets, weren't you? I know you asked your mom to check on me."

"She told you that?"

Ava's brown eyes danced as she nodded.

"Geez." He scrubbed a hand through his hair. Ava was going to think he was a poor, besotted sap. But then his breath stalled.

Ava had stepped close, and she wrapped her arms about him.

"Hugs are allowed?" he whispered, slipping his arms around her.

"Friend hugs."

He chuckled. "What's the difference?"

She drew away just a bit, enough to look up at him. "Oh, there's a difference." She was everything soft and warm against him, and his heart was racing like mad—could she feel that?

"I'm starting to realize that now."

She smiled and released him, stepping away.

"Very short hugs must be friend hugs," he said with a sigh.

She smirked. "Exactly." She picked up her glass of juice again. "So, I decided what I want to do this morning."

Lane eyed her. "Should I be worried?"

"Well, your mom told me that you're quite a horseman, even though you never did much rodeo."

"Not my thing."

"Well, I'm glad it's not your thing," Ava said. "But maybe we can go riding?"

"Do you ride?" Lane asked, trying to hide his surprise. None of her stories had included riding.

"It's been a while, but I've been a few times. With my dad." She shrugged.

But Lane sensed she was blocking some memories. So would riding be a good thing or a bad thing? "That works for me." His gaze trailed the length of her. "I think Evie or Cara have boots around here that you can borrow."

Ava flashed a grin. "Bring them on."

Thirty minutes later, they were cantering on two mares away from the small arena that was part of the ranch. Ava might not have been riding for a while, but she picked things up quickly.

"You're a natural," Lane told her as he rode next to her.

"There's not much to it," Ava quipped.

"Oh really?" Lane shifted closer and nudged her knee with his own. "You're really confident for a newbie."

She met his eyes. "Well, by the end of the week, I'll be racing you. So don't you mouth off to me."

Lane reached for her hand. "I wouldn't dream of it, unless you wanted me to."

"I don't think I'll be asking you that anytime soon..."

She didn't comment on the hand-holding, and they rode in silence for a few minutes, until she said, "This place is beautiful. So peaceful. It's like being in a different world."

Lane nodded. "Agreed. A good world, if it's all you want to see."

The horses' jostling made their hands separate.

"What do you want to see?" Ava asked. "The first place, if you had a choice?"

"I'd probably start with the East Coast," he said. "Never been there. The history of our country is fascinating. I'd be the geekiest tourist."

Ava smiled. "So you're a history junkie?"

"Not really, just feel like I've been a textbook student most of my life." He motioned toward the wide blue sky. "Texas feels so big sometimes that it's hard to imagine the world being even bigger."

Ava's phone rang somewhere in her pocket.

"We can stop if you need to get that."

"Oh, it's probably my mom." She sighed. "I guess talking to her twice yesterday wasn't good enough. And she doesn't like texting much."

"There's a stream up ahead," Lane said. "The horses could use a break anyway."

"All right."

They headed for the stream, and after Lane dismounted, he helped Ava. He released her quickly, because being alone with her, this close, and touching her was quite tempting. He walked to the stream and gazed at the burbling water.

Ava joined him, standing a couple of feet away. "So peaceful out here."

Her phone rang again, and she pulled it out, but canceled the call. "Yep. It's my mom."

"What will you tell her?" he asked, because he really wanted to know.

"Um, just what I already did. I'm sticking to my story." She smiled over at him. "That I'm here with a friend named

Lane Prosper. Taking a break—a vacation—but also job searching online. Although that hasn't happened yet."

"Well, if you'd have gotten up a little earlier."

Ava scoffed. "Are you going to be like this all week? Harassing me about my sleep?"

"No." Lane moved closer to her. "You can sleep as much as you want."

"Oh, well, thank you for the permission, sir." She nudged him.

Not expecting it, Lane shifted his balance and accidentally stepped in the stream.

"Oh, sorry."

"It's fine." Then he turned and grabbed her, pulling her with him into the water.

She screamed, then started laughing. Her back to him, he held her against his chest. She stomped in the water with her boots, splashing both of them good.

"You're just getting yourself wet."

"It's worth it," she said, still laughing. She finally wriggled out of his grasp and stepped onto the bank. Then she sat down in the grass and tugged off her boots.

Lane did the same, out of breath, and half wet. "You're nuts, you know that?" He lay back in the sun-warmed grass. With the early summer heat, they'd be dry in no time.

"No, you're nuts," Ava said, flopping back as well. "You will never win in a water fight against me."

Lane chuckled and turned his head. "Is that a dare?"

Ava turned her head to look at him. "Take it how you will. But if my phone had gotten ruined, you'd be out like hundreds of dollars."

"Did it get wet?"

She pulled her phone out of her pocket. "Nope, still good." As if on cue, it rang again. "Wow. My mom... Hello?"

Take a Chance

Lane wondered if he should take a walk, give her some space, but Ava smiled at him. So he stayed.

"Oh, I slept in, and now we're riding horses . . . Yeah, *we* as in me and Lane. Yep, that boy." She looked over at him and winked. "We're friends, Mom, just like I told you . . . No, Brady and I are done, one hundred percent."

"I'm gonna take a walk," Lane whispered.

But Ava grabbed his hand before he could get up. So he settled back down. And she didn't release his hand as she kept talking to her mom. When she finally hung up, she turned on her side to face him.

"My mom's not buying that we're just friends. So she's worrying that I'm off with some boy, and I'm about to get my heart broken again."

"You should have told her that you're going to be the one breaking hearts, not me."

Ava smiled. "Yeah. That would go over well. But the funny thing is that I never really felt heartbroken over Brady. I was more mad than anything—not even at him, at myself."

Lane nodded. "It's not your fault he was and is a jerk. Good riddance to him."

With a sigh, Ava turned his hand over, then traced a finger across his palm. "My mom knows me too well. Even over the phone. She knows that something's up."

"Is something up?" Lane asked, having a hard time keeping the hope out of his voice.

"I'm having a good time, I guess." She turned and lay on her back again. "I don't remember the last time I did absolutely nothing."

Lane gazed up at the sky. "Same." The sound of the water rippling just beyond them and the warm sun above were definitely a relaxing combination. But he couldn't totally relax, especially if he thought Ava might change her mind about their friendship. "Hey, I need to tell you something."

"A deep secret?"

"Sort of. I mean, you're the only one I'm telling right now."

This had her attention, and she turned toward him again.

He shifted, too, moving up on an elbow. "I got a job offer the other day. On my drive before your concert."

"Oh wow, that's great."

"It's in North Carolina." Lane didn't know if the way her face fell made him happy or not.

"Oh. That's a ways away from Texas."

"Yeah."

"On the East Coast, though," she said brightly. "Think of all the historic places you'll be close to."

"Yeah."

She nudged his foot. "What? Isn't it a good offer?"

"It's a great offer," he said. "Top pay. Excellent company. I'll get promoted pretty fast, too, since the guy above me is retiring in a few months."

"Lane." She sat up. "When we first talked about what you wanted in a job, you wanted to travel. This will get you out of Texas and into a new location. And you'll have money to travel on weekends or take great vacations."

Lane sat up, too, and looped his arms over his bent knees. "Three days ago, I would have agreed. Three days ago, I would have accepted it on the spot."

Ava sighed and dropped her head. "Don't say that, Lane."

"It's the truth, Ava," Lane said. "I'm trying to talk myself out of a lot of stuff right now, believe me."

Chapter 16

Lane's mom had been right, Ava decided. Lane was a serious guy. He thought through stuff. He considered things from all angles. He wasn't spontaneous, and she guessed that the two most spontaneous things he'd ever done in his life were when he'd come to her concert and when he'd invited her to Texas.

But right now, Ava couldn't do serious. She needed time. Time to think. Time to get to know this guy better. He couldn't throw away a perfectly good and amazing job offer because they were attracted to each other.

After they'd ridden the horses back to the ranch, they'd climbed into Lane's truck and headed into the town of Prosper. The place was tiny, charming, and felt like stepping back in time a few centuries.

"There's a real barber shop here?" Ava asked, peering out the passenger-side window.

"Yep." Lane pointed up ahead. "That used to be a general store back in the early days of the state."

Ava laughed. "Oh, there's a bar—or is it a saloon?"

"Depends on who you ask."

"Racoons? Does that name have any significance?"

"You know, I never asked." Lane drummed his fingers on the steering wheel.

Ava noticed he did that a lot. When they weren't holding hands, that was. "Maybe because it's open until the racoons start crowing."

Lane laughed. "You're probably right. We should go there tonight. They usually have karaoke or something going on."

"Oh, so you sing, too?" Ava teased. "You happen to write your own songs, and now you sing?"

"Not really." Lane turned onto a road branching off Main Street. "Just to get out from the watchful eyes of the parents who are asking you incessant questions."

"I don't mind, really," Ava said. "Your parents have only good intentions. For you."

"Uh-oh, what did my mom say to you?"

Ava grinned. "You'll find out if I decide you'll find out." She looked up at the house Lane had slowed in front of.

"Is this Holt's place?"

"Yep." Lane turned off the truck, and just like he'd been doing since they met, he opened her door for her.

His hand lingered on her back as they headed up the walkway to the front door. Then he dropped his hand as he moved to knock quietly. "Baby might be sleeping," he whispered.

So, Lane Prosper was kind of adorable, too. Adorable and serious.

Holt answered the door and motioned for them to come in. In one arm, he held a tiny, wrapped bundle.

"Oh, is that him?" Ava whispered.

"This is Lucas," Holt said with a smile.

Lane shut the door, then moved to stand by them as they all gazed down at the sleeping infant.

"He's so tiny," Ava said. "So sweet."

"He'd better be tiny," a woman said. "He was inside of me three days ago."

Ava turned to see a woman who must be Macie walking into the room. She had a hand on her back and walked slowly, but her smile lit up the room. She definitely looked like little Ruby, with her brown eyes, brunette hair, and honey-colored skin.

"Macie." Lane gave her a gentle hug. When he released her, he said, "This is Ava."

"Hi, Ava." Macie grasped her hand and squeezed. "Great to finally meet you."

"Oh, it's great to meet you, too," Ava said. "And your baby—wow, he's so adorable."

"Thanks," Macie said.

Holt looked over at his wife. "Are you sure you should be up? I got this."

"I'm good." She moved past him, trailing her fingers along his arm. "Just want to see people for a minute."

Holt chuckled. "Okay, but if you get tired, then I can do whatever you need—"

"He fusses too much," Macie said. "Drives me crazy."

But her wide smile told Ava otherwise.

"Do you want to hold him?" Holt asked Lane.

"Sure." Lane took the bundle, carefully and slowly.

Ava was impressed as he rocked the baby.

"You're a pro," Macie said from where she'd settled on the couch. "I guess you're going to be the babysitter."

"Yeah, maybe that will talk you into sticking around." Holt clapped a hand on Lane's shoulder.

Lane looked up. "Hey, don't mix business with pleasure. Right now, I'm enjoying spending time with my new nephew."

"All right, all right." Holt raised his hands, then sat by his wife. They held hands, and Macie leaned her head against his shoulder.

They made a sweet picture, the pair of them.

"Wanna hold him?" Lane asked.

Ava blinked. "Uh, sure." She held out her arms while Lane placed the warm bundle in them. She couldn't remember the last time she'd held a baby, and never a newborn. "Wow, he's so small, yet solid." She swayed from side to side, how she'd seen Lane doing it. The baby wasn't fussy—heck, he was sound asleep—but it felt like the right thing to do while holding him.

"Everything about him is so tiny," Ava marveled. "Even his eyelashes."

"Right?" Macie said. "You should see his toes. Like buttons."

Ava lifted her gaze and smiled at her. "Can I?"

"Sure."

Ava untucked the blanket at the baby's feet until one foot was exposed. "Oh wow, you're right. Tiny. So cute." She felt Lane's gaze on her, but Ava didn't look over at him.

There had already been a lot of emotions going on between them today. She didn't need to see what he saw when she was holding his nephew in her arms. "Hey, little Lucas, what are you dreaming about?"

Everyone chuckled.

"I'm pretty sure he's dreaming about his next feeding time," Holt said. "He was up half the night."

Macie yawned as if on cue. "I agree."

"You can take a nap, darlin'," Holt said. "I'll wake you if he gets hungry."

Ava assumed this meant Macie was breastfeeding the baby.

"We should let you guys rest," Lane said. "We just wanted to stop by for a peek."

Holt rose from the couch and the two brothers hugged.

"I'll head over to the ranch in a couple of hours, and we can go over the spreadsheets," Holt said.

"Sounds good," Lane said.

Ava wouldn't have minded staying longer. Holding a newborn was a surreal experience. To think of the entire lifetime this child had ahead of him, and it had only just begun. She could easily stare at his tiny features all day. By the time they left, Ava was already missing holding the baby.

They grabbed some lunch at the Main Street Diner, where multiple people greeted Lane, and he introduced Ava to them. Everyone asked if he'd moved back, and he had to explain over and over that he was job hunting. It seemed Ava was the only one he wanted to know about his job offer in North Carolina.

Ava felt flattered, but it had become a growing weight between them. Having this solid offer only made their time together seem like it was on a downward slide.

When they headed back to the ranch, Ava took in the sights that she'd seen going the other direction. The wide-open space was inspiring, but she could see how Lane found it constricting as well. You'd have to love the rancher life to be happy in a place like Prosper.

Lane's phone started buzzing again, but since they weren't on a road trip, he didn't ask Ava to read the messages. When they pulled up to the ranch house, he looked at his phone. "Evie says she and Carson will go to Racoons tonight—if we want to go?"

Ava smirked. "Sounds like it's already a plan. When did you ask Evie?"

"When you were holding Lucas."

"I'm good with it," Ava said with a shrug. It would be an experience, if nothing else. Although it meant they'd just be surrounded by more people. Why was she thinking this way, though? She couldn't hog him all the time, and she shouldn't want to.

"Okay, great." Lane looked over at her. "What do you want to do while Holt and I meet?"

"I'll probably practice the piano," Ava said. "Unless you think it will bother your mom?"

"She'll love it," Lane said. "She plays some, but never really got any of her kids too invested in playing the piano, as you've seen with my impeccable nursery rhyme songs."

"Well, it all transferred to the guitar."

Lane shook his head with a smile, then opened his door.

Once again, he was to her side of the truck before she got her seat belt undone. She turned to slide out and he grasped her hand. But when she was on the ground, he didn't let go.

She looked up at him. "You don't always have to open the door for me, you know."

His blue eyes studied her. "What if I want to?"

The Texas sun seemed to intensify, warming the air between them. "I guess you can, but I'm just saying that you don't have to."

His thumb moved over her fingers, and her pulse reacted. Standing this close to Lane, being able to breathe in his scent of cotton and fresh air, only made her realize that she didn't want this week to end anytime soon.

She didn't move, and he didn't, either.

"Thanks for coming home with me," he said in a quiet voice.

Ava's heart felt like it had moved to her throat. "Thanks for inviting me."

He seemed to be leaning a little closer, but she didn't mind.

"Your family's great," she said.

Lane nodded. "What about me? Am I great?"

Take a Chance

Ava laughed and patted his chest with her free hand. "Yeah, you're kind of great, too." It would be so easy to kiss him right now, but that would only torture her later, when she had to say goodbye to him. "I should head in to practice."

He gazed at her for a moment, then released her hand. She stepped past him, and he shut the truck door. Walking toward the house, she wondered if his mom was inside, and if she'd seen them holding hands. It would be hard to explain that they were still just friends.

"You're back already?" Heidi asked, coming out of the kitchen when Ava walked inside with Lane. Beyond her, the kitchen table was covered in rolled-out dough. "I was just getting rolls set up for dinner."

"I can help you," Ava said. "I was going to practice, but this looks like a big job."

"It's nothing," Heidi said. "Everyone's coming for dinner tonight, although, I'll run the leftovers to Holt and Macie's. You go ahead and practice. I'd love to hear you."

"All right." She glanced at Lane, who'd crossed to the kitchen counter and was sampling something out of a bowl.

"Stay out of the cookie dough," Heidi said with a laugh. She turned her blue eyes on Ava. "Some things never change."

Lane winked, then washed his hands.

Ava wandered over to the piano. Running through a few scales, it was quickly obvious that the piano was off-tune, but not terribly. She could deal with it.

When she finished the first set of scales, she skipped to a piece she'd learned only a few weeks ago. She had the first couple of pages memorized, but would have to learn the rest back in Arizona since she hadn't brought her music with her. When she finished, she shifted to another round of scales, and that's when she realized she had an audience. She looked over her shoulder to see Heidi and Lane.

"Too loud?" she asked.

"It's perfect," Lane said.

Heidi glanced at her son. "I guess classical music has now been introduced to the ranch."

"Yes, ma'am."

Heidi's smile was as wide as the Texas sky. "Proceed, my dear. We're all ears." She settled on the couch, and Lane perched on the end of it.

So Ava dove back in, her heart pounding this time. She finished the scales, then reviewed an older piece, one that had plenty of energy to it. On the last stanza, someone started clapping.

"Whoa, that was incredible." Holt had walked into the house without Ava noticing it.

"Thank you." Her voice was breathless, and for some reason, she felt more nervous than she had at the competition the other day in front of an entire auditorium of people. "I can take a break if you need to do your meeting in here?"

"We're headed to the barn office," Holt said. "Proceed, though. We can wait a bit." He threw a wink at Lane.

"Fine with me," Lane said with a smile, folding his arms.

Ava went through another three numbers before the brothers left for their meeting. Heidi stayed on the couch, completely ignoring the dough stretched on the kitchen table. Finally, having played for a good hour, Ava turned and said, "How about I help you with the rolls, then I'll practice some more?"

Heidi gave a little shake of her head. "All right, but only if you want to."

Chapter 17

Ava hadn't ever been into the bar scene, but Racoons was more like a hometown hangout. The bar served up drinks right and left, and the dancing in the middle of the floor was in full swing by the time Ava arrived with Lane, Evie, and Carson.

"We'll grab a table," Evie said, tugging Ava with her. "You guys get the drinks."

Ava didn't complain. She liked how friendly Evie was—it made it easy to hang out with her.

"So . . ." Evie said, once they sat in a round booth, leaving both sides open for the men. "You and Lane, huh? Mom told me you have him mesmerized."

"Just my music," Ava said, her face heating up. "That's how we met and, uh, connected."

Evie's brows tugged together. "Ava, you seem like a smart lady, but in this you are kind of clueless. My brother has never brought home a girl. He's never even *discussed* a girl with any of us, except to say he had a 'one-and-done date.'"

Ava cringed. "Yeah, he told me about those. I thought he was a player."

Evie laughed at this. "It might sound bad, but for Lane, it was simply a date that didn't go anywhere. On any level. He's way too serious to date continually for fun."

"He corrected me pretty quickly."

Evie grinned. "I'm glad you like him, too, because it would be really awkward if it were one sided."

"We're friends—"

"Stop. No rhetoric at a bar. It's a thing, you know. We drink and confess our hearts."

When Ava frowned, Evie continued, "Don't worry, we go non-alcoholic, but in keeping with the theme of any bar, we say it like it is. So don't try to tell me you and Lane are just friends. A sister knows these things about her brother."

Ava kind of wished she and Lane had come alone. Evie was sure persistent. She leaned in toward Ava. "You know, Carson was my first kiss. True story. Made it through high school and college without kissing a single guy."

"Well, that's something."

Evie laughed. "Yeah, it was something." Her gaze shifted to where Carson and Lane were heading over, each carrying two drinks in hand—which looked like soda.

Yeah, Carson was a good-looking man. Dark hair, warm eyes, easy smile, but he was nothing compared to Lane, at least in Ava's mind. She'd take her blond cowboy any day.

"Here you go, ladies," Carson said, setting down the drinks. "Hope you like Shirley Temples."

"Love them," Evie said, scooting a little more so Carson could sit next to her.

Lane slid into the booth next to Ava. "What do you think of Racoons?" he asked, his voice low next to her ear.

Carson and Evie were already caught up in their own conversation.

"It's really hoppin'," she said. "I'm surprised at how many people are here."

Lane smelled pretty divine. He'd obviously used some sort of cologne, although Ava didn't mind his regular clean-cotton scent. He was so close to her that his leg pressed against hers, and his arm brushed hers as he reached for his glass.

"It is karaoke night, so that's the big draw around here." Lane took a swallow of his drink. "Half of these people are from surrounding towns."

"Oh, I was wondering about that," Ava said. "It seemed a lot for Prosper, unless it's the only thing to do."

Lane chuckled. "Well, there's that, too."

"So, did the meeting with Holt go well?" They hadn't had time to talk about it because Evie and Carson had showed up to help with dinner preparations before the meeting was over. And they'd ridden over to the bar with them, too.

"Yeah, it was fine. Good stuff, but let's forget all that for now. Wanna dance?"

Before she could explain that she'd never country-danced in her life, Lane had threaded his fingers through hers. Across the table, Evie noticed. Her brows popped up, and Ava was pretty sure she was going to break out into a blush.

Lane stood, pulling her with him. What the heck, she decided. Maybe it would be fun. But the line dance had ended, and a slow, mellow country tune now blared from the speakers on either side of the small stage.

Lane led her by the hand to the center of the dance floor. Couples filled in the spaces around them. Ava stepped into his arms easily, too easily. His right hand rested on the small of her back, and his left hand clasped her right hand. She slid her other hand over his shoulder, and her fingers brushed the warm skin of his neck just above his collar.

She lowered her fingers because her pulse was already skipping plenty of beats. The slow music, the low lights, and the heat between their bodies only made Ava's thoughts go in a completely wrong direction. Thoughts of moving to North Carolina. They had plenty of university music programs there, right? Although the out-of-state tuition would be out of control.

She refocused her thoughts. She'd be done with school in another year . . . Maybe they could keep a long-distance relationship through that year? It wasn't like she'd want to be too serious anyway with a guy. She was too young to settle down. Just because it *felt* good to be around Lane—and his family was amazing, and he was considerate, funny, loyal, the perfect gentleman—didn't mean he was her one and only.

The song ended way too fast. Ava wasn't finished dancing with this man—as friends—when someone spoke into a microphone.

"Welcome, folks! Up next is karaoke. Line up and choose your songs. We're starting out with Paige Dempsey."

A woman of an uncertain age hopped up on the stage and took the microphone in hand.

"That's our cue," Lane said, steering her toward the bar.

"Cue for what?"

"Signing up for karaoke."

She tugged on his hand. He stopped and turned, his smile mischievous.

"You're singing, then? Because I'm not."

"There's a piano on stage," Lane said. "You can play something. Everyone will love it."

Ava blinked hard. "You can't be serious." She'd seen the piano on the stage, facing backwards and shoved against the wall. It looked like it had fallen off a semitruck at some point.

"I'm dead serious, Ava. The winner's pot is a thousand dollars. You'll win. Why do you think the place is so crowded tonight? High stakes."

"This is a contest?"

"Yep."

Ava looked over at the stage. Paige Dempsey was singing a rather high-pitched rendition of how it was five-o'clock somewhere. "But I'm not from here. I'd be an interloper."

"It's open to anyone." Lane's hand rested on her shoulder, warm and solid.

When his fingers brushed against her neck, she almost gave in.

"I don't play anything contemporary or country, and that's what will win this crowd over."

"What about that first piece you played at the ranch? It would wow this crowd."

Ava bit her lip, gazing into Lane's earnest blue eyes. A thousand dollars was nothing to sniff at. Still . . . "On one condition."

His brows lifted. "Anything."

"You come up with me," she said. "There's a guitar on top of the piano."

Lane's hand dropped. "Uh, no. You're the musician, sweetheart."

She flat out ignored the endearment stirring the butterflies in her stomach. She moved in close, almost as close as they had been while dancing. "Fine. Lost opportunity. I guess we'll just drink Shirley Temples all night."

Lane gazed down at her, and she could almost see the argument marching across his face. "Let's do it."

"Wait, really?" Now that he'd agreed, Ava's pulse skyrocketed.

"Come on." His hand grasped hers again, and she followed him to the bar. They signed up, with only five people ahead of them.

"Why aren't there more if the winner gets a thousand bucks?"

"Because everyone will size up their competition, then decide on a song after they've heard the first few."

"Ah." It sort of made sense. "Imagine, strategy at karaoke night in Prosper, Texas."

Lane grinned. "You got that right, sweetheart."

He'd called her sweetheart twice in one night. Ava didn't know how she felt about that. Well, she knew, but she shouldn't like it this much.

They were headed back to the table, still holding hands. It didn't matter now if Evie saw them—she'd seen enough, Ava guessed. Besides, the place was crowded, and they kept getting jostled. So hanging onto Lane was a good thing.

They slid into the booth.

"So?" Evie said. "You got a spot?"

"Coming up in a few," Lane said.

Evie grinned. "I can't wait to hear you, Ava." She nestled closer to Carson, who had his arm around her.

Ava only smiled, then nudged Lane. He said nothing about him signing up, too. So it looked like his sister would be in for a surprise.

The next few songs went by way too fast, and when it reached the fourth performer, a young man with a cowboy hat that looked older than the entire state of Texas, Ava's nerves climbed up her throat. Good thing she didn't have to sing. Her hands usually didn't shake when she performed, but it wasn't like she'd be playing a memorized piece. She'd be jamming with Lane.

"Am I following you, or are you following me?" she asked him in a low tone.

He was holding her hand under the table, but Ava knew they weren't fooling anyone. "Either way."

Ava thought for a moment. "I'll follow you. It's your town. Your bar."

Lane's mouth curved. "Sure thing, if you insist."

The young man finished his song up on stage, then tipped his hat to the cheering crowd. He'd been decent, and Ava would pick him as the top performer so far. This meant she and Lane had their work cut out for them.

"Show time," Lane said, moving out of the booth.

Ava rose next to him.

"Wait, are you both going up there?' Evie asked.

"Sure thing," Lane said.

They headed to the stage together just as their names were announced. "Next up, Ava Sampson and Lane Prosper. Let's give them a warm welcome, folks."

Scattered applause sounded, and Lane hopped up on the stage, then extended his hand to Ava. "Let's get the piano turned," he said.

Together, they turned the piano so Ava had room to sit in front of it. Then Lane picked up the guitar and began to tune it.

Ava ran a scale. The sound was rough, but it would have to do.

She glanced over at the audience. Curiosity marked several faces. Evie and Carson had joined the dance floor crowd.

"Ready?" Lane asked.

She nodded.

Lane moved the microphone closer to the piano, then he spoke to the audience. "This is instrumental, friends. So listen with an open mind."

A couple of whistles sounded, along with a few groans.

Ava tried not to let the naysayers bother her. This was all in good fun anyway. Win or lose, she'd never forget the sight of Lane plucking out a tune on an old guitar, his blue eyes smiling at her. He played a couple of stanzas before she caught on. It was a slow melody, and she could embellish. Not as great as he could, but hers was the background anyway.

Lane switched keys and tempos. Same song, different flavor.

Ava adjusted, adding in a few more dynamics and crescendos.

When Lane began to taper off, Ava threw in a concluding set of chords, then a couple of trills.

The bar was silent as Ava stood. Lane stepped back from the microphone and nodded over at her.

Then the applause burst. Hooting, whistling, and stamping.

Ava's heart shot to her throat, and she laughed.

"Thank you all," Lane said, leaning forward and speaking into the microphone. "We'll be here all night."

More applause. A few chanted, "One more song."

But Lane set the guitar on top of the piano, then grasped Ava's hand. "Nicely done, sweetheart."

She beamed up at him. "You were the show, hot stuff."

His smile grew. Before he could say anything, Evie and Carson reached them.

"What the heck was that, you guys?" Evie gushed. "Wow. That was insane!"

Carson held up his phone. "Loading to YouTube now."

"Wait, what?" Ava asked. *YouTube?*

Lane only shrugged. "Whatever."

Others came up to them, congratulating them and asking how long they'd been performing together. "This was our first time," Lane said.

People laughed because they thought he was kidding.

When they sat in their booth again, it was a long time before Ava's heart calmed down.

Then, it soared again.

"Ladies and gentlemen," the MC said into the microphone. "We have a winner for tonight's pot of one thousand big ones. Give it up for Ava Sampson and Lane Prosper!"

Ava might have screamed. They jumped up from the booth and headed toward the stage. The crowd parted, clapping, cheering.

One guy in a black hat lunged toward Ava. "You single, lady?"

She laughed him off and slipped her arm through Lane's, sticking close.

"Here ya go." The MC handed down an envelope from where he stood on the stage.

Lane took the envelope. "Thank you, sir."

"Yes, thank you so much," Ava called above the noise.

The music had started again, blaring from the speakers, and a line dance was forming.

"Here you go, sweetheart, all yours." Lane held out the envelope to Ava.

"We're splitting it, dummy."

"Nope." He folded it, then tucked it into her front jeans pocket.

She stared at Lane for a second while people danced around them, shifting them closer to the stage as the music thumped through the room. Then, Ava moved a hand behind his neck and pressed her mouth against his.

She'd surprised him, that was clear, but it was only seconds before he recovered. Drawing her tightly against him, he kissed her back, thoroughly, and in front of at least a hundred people.

Chapter 18

Lane didn't want to open his eyes, because once he did, the new day would be here, and the magic of the night before faded. Ava had kissed him. Yeah, a lot of stuff had happened before that, but the kiss had been the pinnacle.

And it wasn't only in the middle of the bar, but after they'd gotten home. They'd dropped off Carson, then Evie had headed inside the ranch house. Lane and Ava had lingered on the wide porch, and she'd slipped her arms about him, then tugged him close.

An invitation he was happy to accept.

Was it possible to fall for someone in less than a week?

They *had* spent a lot of time together. They'd talked about most subjects from A to Z, and still hadn't run out of things to say. He'd told her about the job offer. She knew there might be more than one state between them. Yet, she'd kissed him.

The smell of bacon was what finally opened his eyes.

He was hungry. Burned every last calorie last night, and then some.

Was Ava awake yet? Was she remembering last night, too?

With a smile? Or did she regret things in the light of a new day?

Lane groaned. *Please, no,* he mouthed. He didn't want to return to the friend zone. So what if they were at his family's home and they all watched him go nuts over a girl? He didn't care what they thought; he only cared what Ava thought.

So, what did *she* think?

He reached for his cell and texted her. It was safer than stepping out into the hallway, where he might run into his mom or dad, and then have to figure out when he could see Ava alone.

Was she in the kitchen? Did she even have her phone with her?

Good morning, Ava. Just checking on our relationship status, because last night was way out of the friend zone.

Nothing like laying it all on the line.

He watched the three dots of her returning text dance for a couple of seconds. He'd never felt so on edge about something in his life.

I'm up for negotiation.

"Yes!" Lane whisper-yelled. Then he typed: *Just a heads up, I might drive a hard bargain. But I need food first for strength. Meet in the kitchen? Someone's cooking.*

Three dots danced again. *That would be me.*

Lane was so there. He straightened his bed, then headed into the bathroom to wash up. He'd shower later—he didn't want to delay any longer. Even if his parents were in the kitchen, too. But he found only Ava standing at the stove, flipping pancakes.

She hadn't exactly dressed yet, and wore what he'd seen her in that morning in her apartment. Cut-off sweats that served as shorts, and an oversized T-shirt. Her sleeve had slipped down one shoulder.

"What's this?" he asked. "Someone's cooking up heaven."

Ava's smiling brown eyes met his, and he wrapped his arms around her from behind. She leaned against him, and he kissed her bare shoulder.

This was nice, very nice.

"What happened?" he asked. "You're up early."

"Didn't sleep much," she said. "And I was starving, so when I heard your dad moving about the kitchen, I came in. Asked if I could fix him something more than the coffee and toast he was making. Didn't turn me down."

Lane chuckled. "Smart man."

"Your mom already ate, too. They had an appointment, I guess, in San Antonio?"

He sobered. "I think it's her blood draw at a clinic there. She goes once a month."

At this, Ava set down the spatula and turned in his arms. Looping her arms about his neck, she asked, "Are you worried? She seems pretty healthy."

"Well, it's just a precaution, but it's a worry until I hear otherwise."

Ava nodded. "I'm glad she's getting checked so regularly."

"Me, too." Lane pulled her in closer. "So . . . change of subject . . ."

Her mouth curved. "Which subject are we on now?"

"*Us.* And the fact that we're alone in the house." He leaned closer, testing. When she didn't draw away, he closed the distance and kissed her. She tasted like syrup. "Hey. You already ate?"

She laughed. "Um, yeah. Like I said, I was starving. You're the one who slept in."

"Mmm." He kissed her again, lingering this time. Her fingers moved into his hair, and he shifted her away from the hot stove until they were against the counter.

"The stove's on," she whispered.

He reached toward the stove and turned off the element. Didn't need anything to catch on fire—more than what was already burning between him and Ava.

Their kissing slowed and became exploratory. When Ava tugged up his shirt and her hands slid along his skin, he knew they needed to cool things.

When he broke off, she was breathless.

"Babe," he whispered. "I really like kissing the cook in the kitchen, but I want to do this right. Between us. Which means..."

"Which means?" she prompted with a sweet smile.

"That we take it down a notch, for now."

"Okay."

"Okay?"

She nodded and set her hands over his, which were anchored on her hips. "You're right. Besides, we're in your parents' house. And you're probably going to be moving to North Carolina—"

"About that," he cut her off. "I'm not taking the job."

Her eyes widened. "Lane. You can't turn it down just because—"

He kissed her firmly. "It's not because of you, or us, it's because..." He hadn't really expected to have this discussion this morning, but moving to North Carolina would seriously curtail whatever was happening between him and this woman. "Okay, you're right. It's you. Us. Whatever *this* is. I'm not going to move across the country and maybe see you, what? Once a month? Every couple of months?"

"Lane," she chided softly.

"I like you, Ava. More than I've ever liked anyone I've ever met, or am related to, probably. Don't tell my mom."

She smiled, but her eyes were watery.

"There's a reason we met on my graduation day," Lane said. "Before it was too late."

"Too late?"

"Too late to take a chance with you." He grasped both of her hands and linked their fingers. "There are other jobs, but there aren't other women."

Ava scoffed. "There are tons of other women."

He released her hands and cradled her face. "Not for me, babe."

A tear fell on her cheek. She reached up to brush it away. "I don't know why I'm crying. I'm fine. You're fine. You're amazing. And I like you, too." She half-laughed, half-sobbed. Then she was hugging him, tightly.

He held her against him and buried his face into her neck, breathing her warm, sweet scent. Definitely maple syrup.

"I can't believe you're going to turn down that job," she murmured. "What if it's the best one out there?"

"Doesn't matter," he said. "I'll be a fantastic hire for whichever company in Arizona decides to take a chance on me."

She lifted her head at that and gazed at him. "Arizona, huh?"

"Why not? I mean, it's just as good as any other state, right?"

Ava smirked. "Right . . ."

"I guess I should ask you if you'd be okay with a boyfriend hanging around?"

She moved her hands up his chest, then over his shoulders. "A boyfriend named Lane Prosper?"

"That would be the one."

She laughed. "I'm in."

"Good."

Then they were kissing again. At some point, Lane would

eat the delicious-smelling breakfast, but Ava had his full attention right now.

"I think someone's here," she whispered against his mouth.

"What?" Sure enough, he heard the rumble of a truck. It wasn't his dad's, though, because that thing was quiet.

Lane reluctantly released Ava and crossed to the window to look out. The tricked-out truck could only belong to one person. "My brother's here."

"Do you have another meeting?"

"Not that brother. It's Knox."

"Oh. I should get dressed. Tell him to help himself to the food. Or, wait, it's your house."

Lane grabbed her hand before she could take off. "You look fine. He's already on the porch."

Sure enough, the clomp of boots announced Knox's arrival. He tapped on the door, then opened it, finding it unlocked.

"Anyone home?" Knox's voice rang out. "I smell something good."

Within seconds, Knox had entered the kitchen. He wore a black hat that made his green eyes seem brighter. He was the shortest of the three brothers, but he had the fierce, wiry strength of a rodeo star.

"Bro, you were amazing last night," Knox said, then his eyes landed on Ava. "You must be the woman who took my brother viral on YouTube." He stuck his hand out to Ava, who shook it, but there was confusion on her face.

"What are you talking about, Knox?" Lane asked.

Knox set his hat on top of the kitchen table, then scrubbed a hand through his dirty-blond hair. "Your little performance at Racoons last night. Evie sent me the link. You two are trending something big." Knox opened a cupboard and grabbed a plate, then started loading it up with pancakes, eggs, and bacon.

Ava pulled out her phone and opened the YouTube app. "What's it called?"

Knox peered over at her. "Uh, just type in both of your names, and it should come up."

Lane moved to stand by Ava as the video came up. Only now did he remember that Carson had said something about videoing their performance, then sending it to YouTube. He'd titled the video "Small-Town Music Sensation: Duo with Lane Prosper and Ava Sampson."

"Oh wow," Ava murmured, pointing at the screen. "Look. Almost a million views, and several hundred comments." She scrolled down, and the comments popped up.

Lane rubbed his chin. "So people liked it?"

From his spot at the kitchen table, Knox said, "If you consider words like 'amazing,' 'we want more,' 'who are these people,' and 'so talented' as compliments, then yeah."

Ava was grinning. "Look at this comment. 'Come play at our music club. We'll pay your expenses.'"

Lane stared at it. "That's probably not real."

Knox had already downed two pancakes. "New recipe by Mom? These are excellent."

"Ava cooked."

Knox locked his gaze on her. "Is that right? Well, thank you, sugar. It seems that you have many talents—music and cooking."

Ava blinked, as if she didn't know how to react to Knox. Finally, she said, "Thanks," then looked back down at her phone.

Just then, the house phone rang. Yeah, Lane's parents still had a landline. Lane crossed to it and answered. "Prosper residence."

"I'm calling for Lane," a man said. "Is he still in town?"

"This is Lane," he said, not recognizing the man's voice. All of his friends or job connections would use his cell number.

"This is Bud at Racoons. Checking in to see how long you and your little lady are hanging around town. I heard that you're in between jobs or something?"

"Sort of." His gaze cut to Ava, who could probably hear most of the conversation since Bud had a rather loud voice. "We're here for a few more days."

"That's great to hear," Bud said. "Now, I called for a favor. But I'm willing to pay, too. Five hundred a night. It's not as much as the winning pot last night—but we only do that once a week. But see here—you guys come and do your thing at Racoons tonight, and I can guarantee that the place will fill up. I've got dozens of comments on my Facebook page and even more direct messages, asking if you two will be back for an encore."

Lane didn't know what to say. He covered the receiver and quickly explained whatever Ava didn't already have the gist of. "What do you think?"

"Five hundred a night?" Knox piped up. "Sounds good in my book."

Lane ignored his brother. "Ava?"

"Sure, why not? Unless we have other plans." She shrugged, but there was a smile on her face.

Lane spoke into the receiver. "Count us in. If tonight goes well, we'll come back tomorrow."

"Excellent," Bud said. "I'll spread the word. Might add a cover charge; if I do, I'll give you guys ten percent of that as well."

"Sounds fine by me." When Lane hung up, he turned to Ava. "Well, that's crazy."

She laughed and hugged him. Which turned into a kiss. Which made Knox say, "Want me to leave?"

They broke apart.

Ava was blushing, and Lane probably was, too. "I'd better get some food before you decide to go for seconds." He grabbed his own plate, filled it up, then sat down across from his brother.

Ava started on the dishes, but Knox stopped her. "Put those down, sugar. You cooked. We'll clean up."

Ava looked from Knox to Lane. "Sounds good." Then she sat right next to Lane. He reached for her hand, no longer worried about PDA, since, well, that kiss had happened in front of Knox.

"Guess I'll be sticking around to watch you two tonight." Knox took a swallow of juice.

"What brings you home?" Lane asked. "I don't remember Mom fussing over your impending arrival."

"It's a surprise," Knox said. "Not for you. For Jana. Finished up a rodeo last night and started driving. Well, and I need some time with Ruby, too. Might as well see her new half-brother." He lifted his hand to stifle a yawn. "Mind if I crash somewhere? Then I'll be more awake to see Jana."

"Sure. Ava's in Cara's room. You can take Holt's."

Knox grunted, then rose to clear his plate. When he turned on the kitchen faucet, Lane said, "I'll do the dishes. You get some sleep."

Knox didn't hesitate. "Thanks, bro." He clapped a hand on Lane's shoulder. "You always were my favorite brother."

Lane scoffed.

After Knox had left the room, Lane turned to Ava. "Sure you're okay with another night at Racoons? This time as the main attraction?"

"Yeah, but we're splitting the money this time," she said. "You can't keep mooching off your parents."

Lane burst out with a laugh.

"Can you keep it down in there?" came a voice from somewhere in the depths of the house.

Ava grinned. "Knox is funny. I don't know what I expected. Maybe more of the strong, silent type, like his other brothers."

"He's a nut, that's what he is." Lane held her gaze. "Are you sure you're not struck down by his charm and good looks? He's the heartthrob of Prosper, you know."

Ava turned fully toward Lane and loosely looped her arms about his neck. "Well, if you dump me, then maybe I'll consider Knox."

"Oh really?"

"No." Ava leaned closer. "Knox might be all that in the rodeo world, but you're all that to me. We're viral now, so that's kind of a big deal."

Lane tugged her chair closer and decided it was a good time to kiss her again.

Chapter 19

Ava's head was spinning. Tomorrow, she'd be heading back to Arizona, and she didn't want to leave—Texas or Lane. Yeah, she missed her mom and Jenni, but Ava didn't feel in any hurry to get back.

But her original week had turned into two weeks, and the plane ticket had been bought. Ava was now questioning why she'd gotten the ticket—well, Lane had paid for it. Ava supposed that both of them were hesitant to take the next step.

Committing as boyfriend and girlfriend had been a pretty big step, but felt right. And every night since that first night at Racoons, they'd played their duo numbers, mostly newly made up, but some repeats. They'd even played in two other bars in neighboring small towns.

Now they were on their way to San Antonio.

To play in a club there.

The invitation had given Ava goosebumps.

This was all happening so fast, and so unexpectedly, that Ava wondered if it was all too good to be true.

Because Ava had amassed over $6,000 now, all in two weeks. If she kept this up the rest of the summer, she'd have school and board fully paid for, and then some.

Lane pulled onto the highway as they left Prosper.

It all felt so bittersweet, especially the goodbyes to his family. His mom had actually cried. Sweet woman. Her bloodwork results had come back clear the other day, and everyone in the family could relax a little longer.

"Are you okay, sweetheart?" Lane asked. "You've sighed a dozen times since we got on the freeway."

Ava looked over to find his blue eyes on her. "Just thinking."

"Uh-oh, should I be concerned?" He cracked a smile.

But she only sighed again. Then she leaned her head on his shoulder because she was sitting in the middle of the bench at his request—it was what girlfriends of cowboys did, apparently. Then she laced their fingers together.

Lane kissed the top of her head, and for a moment, Ava relished this familiarity with him.

She didn't want it to end, that's what she was thinking. Could she say that to him? Would it be too much? Too fast? Too presumptuous?

Maybe not. He was the one who was searching for a job in Arizona near the university.

"Just wishing that tomorrow wasn't already tomorrow."

"Same."

She smiled, but stayed quiet.

"Hey, I was thinking . . ." he began.

"Should I be worried?"

He chuckled. "Depends. It was actually Knox who gave the idea to me. Remember when he called earlier?"

Ava lifted her head. "Yeah, you said he was bugging you about going on the road with our act. But it would take tons of time and coordination to get it set up. And we both can't put off our futures because our YouTube video trends for a couple of weeks."

"Right," Lane said. "But I had another idea after talking to the guy who owns this comedy club. Did some research."

"About what?"

"Well, I looked up the schedule of the club, and they have a traveling act for the summer," Lane said. "They perform for about a week in each place since they have multiple comedians. Then they all rotate to the next location. Kind of like a summer tour."

"So what are you saying?"

"I thought if tonight goes well, and everything clicks with us and the tour manager, maybe we could pitch our idea."

Bubbles of excitement stirred inside of Ava. "And what's our idea?"

"That we tour with them. We become the opening act, or maybe we're the intermission entertainment. Whatever. We can keep making money, but be together. Save up more for your college, and well, if a job comes through, I'll tell them I can start in early September."

Ava stared at Lane's profile. "You'd do that for me?"

"You, me, both of us," Lane said, glancing at her. "It would mean that I wouldn't have to say goodbye to you."

Ava pushed up and kissed his cheek. "I love that idea, although my mom will freak."

"Really? She'd hate it?"

Ava nudged him. "No, I think she'd love it, too. After calling your mom and having that chat, she's been more settled about me being in Texas 'chasing after some boy.'"

Lane chuckled. "I'm glad our moms both got on the same page. If my mom had her way, you'd have a permanent room at Prosperity Ranch."

"And if you had your way?"

His smile grew, and he gave her a sidelong glance. "It would be more than that."

The butterflies in her stomach were back. "Okay, so best case scenario, we tour with this comedy group. Worst case, I fly to Arizona tomorrow."

"Correct."

Ava leaned her head against his shoulder again and sighed. "I hope you play well tonight, because I'm going to kill it."

"That's what I like to hear, sweetheart."

When they arrived at the comedy club after checking into their two hotel rooms, the owner, a guy by the name of JR, welcomed them. He was as tall as Lane, but a wiry guy with the habit of scratching his chin about every other sentence.

They examined the stage, Lane tuned his guitar, and Ava ran some scales on the old-as-the-hills piano. She missed playing the pristine baby grands at the university. But if Lane's idea happened, she'd have to settle for playing whatever piano was around for the rest of the summer.

She wouldn't mind one bit.

"Well, we're sold out tonight," JR said, approaching the two. "Guess the post to our website with your YouTube video link got some interest. Not sure if it's you or the comedian."

"I heard that," another man said, walking into the club. He had a dark beard and laughing brown eyes. "I'm Phil—the bread-and-butter winner around here, although it seems like I owe the pair of you thanks."

Both Ava and Lane shook the man's hand.

"Nice to meet you," Lane said. "Been in the business long?"

"Going on fifteen years," Phil said. "Most of those were pretty lean, but the last couple of years have been much better thanks to JR's idea of a traveling summer tour."

"It's a fabulous idea," Ava said. "Especially as a group—you can get a lot of momentum going."

"That's the plan." JR rubbed at his chin. "Now, it's five minutes until the doors open, so if you don't mind, head on backstage."

Phil walked with them. The backstage area consisted of a hallway with a handful of chairs. "Luxurious, huh?"

Ava laughed, and Lane smiled.

"How long have you two lovebirds been together?" Phil asked.

"A couple of weeks," Lane said.

"No kidding?" Phil looked from one to the other. "So you were friends, fellow musicians for a while, right?"

"No," Ava said. "We literally met two and a half weeks ago."

"Whoa." Phil grinned. "I guess when you click, you click. It's like the universe having a perfect day."

Ava's heart thumped. Phil had come up with the perfect description.

When Phil was called onto stage, he said, "Good luck to you during the intermission performance. I hope I get the crowd nice and eager."

During Phil's performance, laughter rang out regularly, and that was a good thing. They could hear the applause from the audience, but Phil's voice was muffled.

"What do you think?" Lane asked. "Being on the road won't be fancy."

Ava looked over at him. "I'm not really into fancy. Besides, we could travel."

"True." He extended his hand, and when she took it, he tugged her toward him. He pulled her onto his lap, and she looped her arms about his neck.

"I think you should lead tonight," Lane said. "Just like that first time in my old apartment. We're at our best, then. And I think we need to get some outfits that blend."

"Wow, you're full of ideas."

"That was Knox's idea."

"Ah." Ava leaned close and gave him a small kiss. "I like it. I'm not much of a stylist, so maybe your mom can help? She always looks great."

Lane's brows popped up. "My mom would love that." His arms tightened about her. "I think she likes you more than me anyway."

Ava smirked.

The clapping on the other side of the wall grew in volume.

"Is that our cue?" Ava asked.

"Yep."

They stood and walked hand in hand through the door leading to the stage.

Phil introduced them while Lane slipped the strap of his guitar over his head. Phil cracked a couple more jokes, then Lane took the microphone.

"Hello, folks, I'm from down the road in a little rodeo town called Prosper, and my partner here, Ava Sampson, is from Arizona. So let's give her a Texan welcome."

The audience roared with applause and whistles.

Ava waved in acknowledgment, then moved to the piano and settled on the bench.

"Now," Lane continued, "each of our performances are different, and tonight, Ava will be the lead. This means that she'll start playing whichever song she chooses, then I follow along, improvising. Sometimes things get twisted, and our roles switch. But we always hope to deliver a unique musical experience."

More clapping.

Lane put the microphone back on its stand, then turned to Ava and tipped his hat.

She met his blue gaze, smiled, then began the piece that she'd played for the competition.

His eyes widened, then he grinned. She only got a few lines in before he picked up the bass notes with his guitar.

As Ava played, she thought about what would have happened if she'd won the competition. Would she have come to Texas? Would she have ever played at Racoons? Would she have fallen in love with Lane Prosper?

Her heart soared with the music, and her eyes pricked with tears. Yeah, she loved this man who was a few feet away from her, strumming his heart out. And she could only hope that JR would agree to take them on.

The audience gave them a standing ovation after they finished, and Ava took that as an excellent sign.

Another comedian performed the second half of the show, and after most of the guests had left that evening, Lane grasped Ava's hand. "Ready?" His gaze wasn't only asking if she was ready to make a deal with JR, but maybe other things, more personal things between them.

"Yep." And she was.

She didn't care about backstage hallways with cheap plastic chairs, or altering her vision of her future, because she wanted it to be with Lane. And this was where they'd ended up. Together.

"Hey, JR, can we talk business for a moment?" Lane asked when they found him, working on one of the microphones.

JR looked up and scratched his chin. "I prepaid, right? Was it the right amount?"

"Yeah, it's all good." Lane glanced at Ava. "We want to join the tour. We can open, or be an intermission number, or the finale. Whatever."

JR set down the microphone and straightened. He looked from one to the other. "I don't know. There would be added costs with two more people."

Take a Chance

Phil strode up. "I think it's a brilliant idea." He held up his phone. "I recorded their number tonight, and I think if we stick it on YouTube, announce the addition to the tour, we're going to be selling out all across the country."

JR set his hands on his hips. "Can I think about it? I appreciate the interest, Lane and Ava. And thanks for the vote, Phil. I just know that my wife will want to discuss it. She's the accountant, you see, the brains."

Lane nodded. "Of course. You have our cell numbers. We're staying in San Antonio overnight anyway. We could meet in the morning if you want, but we'd like an answer pretty soon. Ava is supposed to fly back to Arizona tomorrow around noon."

"Wait, you're leaving?" Phil asked. "Breaking up the duo?"

"It was planned before"—Ava waved her hand—"all of this. But I'm willing to miss my flight if JR likes our idea."

Everyone focused on JR. He threw up his hands. "I'm gonna think about it, folks. Just gotta talk to my wife."

Lane chuckled. "We'll wait to hear from you."

By the time they reached the hotel, Ava's nerves were tied into a knot. "How long does it take to talk to his wife? He's probably home by now."

Lane draped an arm across her shoulder as they walked along the interior hallway of the hotel. Their rooms were on the same floor. "If he says no, maybe we could set up a tour on our own."

Ava paused in front of her hotel room door. She turned to Lane before opening it. "Are you sure you want to do that? It would be a lot more work, and—"

A kiss stopped her. Well, then. She moved her hands up his chest and pressed closer.

"I'm sure, sweetheart," he murmured, then lifted his

head. His blue eyes were as steady as ever. "More than sure. It will be our Plan B. You should just cancel that flight right now."

Ava's adrenaline zoomed through her veins at that thought of doing this. *Really* committing. "Okay."

"Okay?"

She nodded.

Lane whooped and picked her up, then slowly spun her around. She laughed and grasped his shoulders. Then he lowered her just enough to kiss her. When he set her back on the ground, she was pretty sure she was floating.

"I love you, Lane Prosper." The words had just come out—but now that they were out, she knew she'd never take them back again.

He went still. Then he exhaled slowly. "I love you, too." His hands cradled her face. "So much."

Her heart did a series of jumping jacks as he bent to kiss her again.

His phone rang, but he continued to kiss her, ignoring it.

"Lane, what if it's JR?" she murmured.

"Oh, right." Lane straightened and pulled the phone out of his pocket. "This is Lane . . . Hey, JR . . . Yeah, we're still interested . . . Yep, very serious."

Lane paced away, and Ava folded her arms about her middle, watching and waiting.

He spun, his gaze connecting with hers. "Yes, let me put the phone on speaker so that Ava can hear."

JR's voice came through. "Ava, Lane, I'd like to officially invite you to join the tour. My wife's emailing over the contract. If you agree, then sign, and return it. We leave for Memphis this weekend. Oh, and we're renting a van. Nothing fancy."

Ava smiled at Lane, and he smiled back.

"Thanks, JR," Lane said. "We're very excited and very grateful."

"My wife is, too. I showed her the video on YouTube, and when she saw the sales from tonight, she was convinced."

After they'd hung up with JR, Lane laughed. "I can't believe it."

Ava hugged him tightly. "I can. It's crazy, though." She drew away. "Did I tell you that I love you?"

Lane's smile was soft. "You did, sweetheart. But I'd love to hear it again."

She rose up on her toes and whispered in his ear, "I love you, hot stuff."

Epilogue

Three Months Later

"It's packed," Ava said, coming to stand by Lane backstage at the San Antonio arena.

Her hand slipped into his, and it felt like they'd been holding hands for years, and not for just a few months. Tonight, they matched in royal blue. She wore a knee-length dress that swished as she walked, and he wore a royal-blue shirt with, yes, fringe. Ava had laughed, but then told him she loved it. After all, they were back in Texas now.

"Sure is a full house," Lane said. "They're all here for you."

"Hardly. Miss Rosie is the headliner."

"Yeah, probably. But you're number two."

"Which makes *you* number three?"

Lane chuckled and pulled her into his arms so her back was to him. He rested his chin atop her head—a perfect fit. Miss Rosie had gone viral on YouTube soon after Lane and Ava's debut. Her ventriloquist performance was stellar, and Lane was thrilled to have been invited to this musical bonanza—filled with unique musicians that didn't fit the regular performance mold.

He scanned the arena that was used for either hockey or basketball—yet here they were. Ava was right. The entire place was filled to the nosebleed seats, and the show wasn't starting for another twenty minutes. Summer was almost over, and they'd returned to San Antonio.

It turned out Lane hadn't needed to take a job in North Carolina to see the rest of the country. He'd spent the last few months visiting a dozen states on the comedy tour. Their final performance had been three days ago in Philadelphia. Then, he and Ava had been invited to a music bonanza with other indie musicians, and they'd decided this would be their last performance before heading back to Arizona.

Ava would finish her last year at college, and Lane, well, he was taking a job with a small insurance company—heading up their finances. So he'd be a number cruncher after all. But that would be temporary, he knew, and give him job experience in his field while he waited for Ava to graduate. Then . . . who knew what might happen from there?

For now, though, they were staying on the music train as long as it would last. Ava's tuition for next year had been earned several times over, and Lane had collected his own nest egg.

Throughout their touring that summer, Lane had learned one thing about Ava. She was *it* for him. Now, and always. If she wanted to get a master's degree, he'd relocate to wherever that ended up being. If she wanted to quit this insane music ride they were on, he'd get a more permanent job. If she wanted to get married and have babies, he'd be saying "I do," without hesitation.

Ava pulled his arms more tightly about her, and he inhaled the scent of her shampoo. It changed frequently, according to whichever motel they stayed in. That thought brought a smile to his face. Ava insisted on staying in motels over hotels whenever possible. She wanted to support the smaller businesses, plus didn't want to overpay—even when they could afford it. Lane also knew she'd sent money to her mom a couple of times.

"Do you see them?" Ava asked.

"Who?"

She elbowed him, and he grinned, even though she couldn't see it.

Both of their families were coming tonight. Ava's mom and the entire Prosper family. Well, Cara and Knox were both up in the air when plans were being made on the group text. Lane wouldn't hold it against them if they couldn't make it. Everyone had their own lives, after all.

Ava lifted her arm and pointed. "Oh look, I think that's my mom."

Lane looked in that direction.

"She's wearing a pink sweater. She's ... oh, I think that's the man she's been dating."

Lane spotted a dark-haired woman wearing a pink sweater. She was holding hands with a man a couple inches shorter.

"She looks happy," Ava said. "Don't you think so?"

Ava's mom cast frequent swoony smiles at her date, and when the man motioned for her to enter the aisle of seats before him, she leaned over to kiss his cheek.

"Definitely happy."

Ava sighed. "I'm glad." She paused. "Oh, there's your parents."

Sure enough, not far from the aisle where Ava's mom had entered, the entire Prosper clan was making its way down the steps. Lane had reserved everyone's seats on the third row, giving them the best view of the part of the stage where the piano was set up.

"Well, looks like my brother Knox made it after all," Lane said with a shake of his head.

Ava laughed. "Oh, you mean that guy signing autographs by the portal?"

"That would be him." Knox was clearly with his red-haired fiancée Jana, who stood next to him, but the fangirling around him didn't stop.

Then a tall blond woman stepped between Knox and the teenagers and said something that sent them sulking away.

"Does Knox have security?"

Lane chuckled, his heart expanding. "Nope. That's my sister, Cara. Guess she decided to leave California for a bit."

"Cara?" Ava turned to face him, and Lane dropped his arms. "She came? Wow . . . that's great. I finally get to meet her."

He settled his hands lightly at her hips. "I think she was tired of hearing all about the woman in my life and feeling left out that she was the only one who hadn't met you."

Ava smirked and looked back at the arena.

"Who's that with Cara—her fiancé?"

Lane looked again. "Yep, looks like Roman came with his daughter Mia." He didn't know what he thought about that—he was surprised, that was for sure. His entire family was here, with their significant others. They usually only reunited at Christmastime.

As Knox and Jana made their way down the steps, followed by Cara and her crew, more Prospers arrived. Holt and Macie, holding their baby. Evie and Carter were right behind them, Ruby between the pair, grasping both of their hands.

"I guess our families are finally going to meet," Ava said.

"I guess." He took her hand and squeezed, and she squeezed back.

Being on the comedy/music tour with Ava this past summer had put them in each other's spheres more than if they'd been dating an entire year, or even two. Lane knew all Ava's quirks, dislikes, likes, and loves. And she knew all of his. Yet . . . he found everything adorable about her. Even when she was a little cranky in the mornings. And even when she sometimes preferred practicing her classical music instead of going sightseeing with him. He gave her space, even when he only wanted to be with her.

They were committed to each other, that he knew, but strangely, he wanted more. "Just ask her to marry you," Knox had told him a few nights ago during a late-night phone call. About the only time his brother would return a call.

"It's not that simple," Lane had said. "Marriage is serious business."

Knox knew that better than anyone, and Lane felt like he could talk to his brother, who'd been through a divorce and was currently in a long engagement. Besides, if Lane told Holt or Dad about what was on his mind, everything would be blown out of proportion. As it was, he just wanted to bounce off his thoughts to the most non-threatening person in his family.

"It *is* that simple." Knox had chuckled. "Only four words, in fact. *Will you marry me?* I mean, you can add more—all that lovey dovey stuff. Or shorten it to *marry me*. Might want to add *babe* or *darlin'* at the end of that, though."

Lane had scoffed, but his heart had also raced. He and Ava hadn't ever discussed marriage—at least specific to *them*. She'd only said that her mom had wished she'd dated a lot more before marrying her father.

"Are you okay with meeting my entire family, Ava?" he asked now.

A few other musicians approached the backstage opening to peer at the crowds. They were jostled enough that Lane let go of Ava.

"Wow-ee," a guy with a mustache and a banjo said. "My nerves are climbing my throat." He threw a nod in Lane's direction, then headed back to wherever he'd come from.

Ava looked over at Lane, her brown eyes dark in the shadows of backstage. "I met most of your family two days after I met *you*. I think I can handle Cara and her producer man. What about you? You okay with meeting my mom's boyfriend?"

Lane laughed. "Of course. If your mom approves of me, then I'm not worried about a guy she happens to be dating. Wait, your mom does approve of me, right?"

Ava folded her arms. "I'm not sure actually, she hasn't directly said."

He groaned. Her mom had come to one of their performances midsummer, and they'd all had a nice dinner after with friendly conversation. At least Lane had thought so. But he hadn't been privy to the private conversations between mother and daughter.

"Ava?" He didn't relish the swell of panic that coursed through him. Suddenly, her answer was very, very important.

Her eyes sparked with amusement. "She loves you, dummy."

"You sure know how to give a man a heart attack." Lane closed the two steps between them and cradled her face.

He loved that he could do this—take her in his arms, kiss her, hug her, hold her hand—keep her close.

Her eyes widened, and her voice quieted. "You were worried?"

"A little," he admitted. "I realized I hadn't asked the question before, and then suddenly I wondered—"

She raised up and pressed her mouth to his in a light kiss. "You don't have to worry, hot stuff. My mom is a smart woman and knows I'm a lucky girl."

Lane's mouth curved upward. "Is that so?"

Ava's smirk was adorable. "You don't need to let it go to your head."

"Hmm." Lane leaned close, moving a hand behind her head. Her hair was down tonight, waving in loose curls. "It's hard not to let things you say go to my head. You're beautiful and talented and sweet and—"

"Stop." She laughed and smacked his chest.

They probably only had minutes before the MC started things, but he'd make those minutes great.

He kissed her, because he could, and because he wanted to. He didn't mind the musicians milling about—everyone knew they were a couple. So did his family, and hers. Ava pulled him closer, fitting against him like pieces of a puzzle. He kissed her slowly. There was no rush, after all. Their number wasn't until about halfway through the program.

But finally, she pulled away, her eyes gleaming, her lips red, her breathing shortened.

"You need to save that for later, hot stuff."

"Noted."

Then she kissed him again. Briefly. Too briefly, but it made Lane's pulse skip ahead anyway. Because the idea forming in his mind since he'd witnessed the arrival of both of their families was starting to take root. Maybe the idea had been there much longer, but the pieces hadn't clicked together yet.

Lane could hardly breathe thinking of it. But he had to breathe, or he wouldn't make it through their number.

Take a Chance

The MC's voice boomed on the other side of the stage and the arena broke out into applause and cheers. From there, it was one musical performance after another, and the audience ate everything up.

Ava left his side when she had a phone call come in and had to find a quieter place.

Lane peeked through the partitions more than once to spy on his family. He smiled when he saw that Ruby and Mia were in cahoots with each other. Clapping at the same time. Excitedly talking to each other. Laughing together. The two girls were cute.

"Hey, the chair of the music program just called me back," Ava said, joining his side again.

"Oh, what did he say?"

"He's approving that I can do all my classes Monday through Wednesday," she said, her eyes bright. "That way Thursday and Sundays can be travel days, and we can perform Fridays and Saturdays."

They'd talked about continuing to play at gigs during the fall, but only if it worked with Ava's schedule. Lane had already gotten permission from his upcoming job to work remote a couple days a week.

"That's fantastic," he said, hugging her.

She laughed. "I know. I mean I had my doubts—but I think he said yes because Thursday and Friday are usually practice or workshopping days."

"That, and you're amazing, and encouraging tons of people to love classical music again."

"Maybe."

He squeezed her again, then kept her close. "You gonna lead tonight?"

"Sure."

"Perfect."

And that's when the MC announced their names. "Next up we have Ava Sampson and her cowboy, Lane Prosper. Let's give a hearty welcome to this piano-guitar duo."

Cheering echoed through the arena. Lane thought it was a bit cheesy to be introduced as a cowboy in Texas, but whatever.

He tightened his hold on Ava's hand, and they walked out together. His gaze immediately went to his family's location. Knox had his fingers to his lips, blowing a long whistle. Ruby and Mia were on their feet, grinning and clapping. The rest were more subdued, staying in their chairs and clapping.

Lane flashed them a wink, then let go of Ava's hand and stepped up to the mic. Ava had insisted he do all the mic talking. She didn't want to deal with the audience.

"Good evening, folks," Lane said. "It's a privilege to be back in my home state. I'd like to recognize my family and Ava's family, who are in attendance tonight. Some of them from different states."

More clapping and cheering sounded in the arena.

"Mostly, I'd like to recognize this music bonanza and the platform it gives indie music artists like me and Ava."

More cheering.

Ava plucked out a few chords.

"Looks like Ava's leading tonight," Lane said with a laugh. "We'll see if I can keep up. Welcome to the ride, everyone!"

He stepped back as the arena filled with clapping.

Ava struck another chord, and Lane adjusted his guitar. He was starting to feel nervous—not about the performance, but about something else. Looking over at Ava and her elegant form and focus on the piano, his throat tightened. Emotions charged through him. He loved this woman, had for a while.

Probably since the moment they'd first kissed in his college basement apartment.

But that was nothing compared to how he felt about her now. He'd told her, of course, and she'd said it back, but it didn't seem enough. Not anymore.

Lane realized she'd played a couple of stanzas, and he was just staring at her.

She glanced over at him, her brows furrowed.

Swallowing, he started in with the bass, always an easy follow-along. Then she picked up a melody he'd heard her practice a couple of weeks ago, although he hadn't asked the name of the piece. He switched keys and continued to follow her lead.

The tune was jaunty, and the audience began to clap in time. This only made Ava play faster. Lane increased his own speed to keep up. He swore he heard Knox whistling again.

Finally, Ava slowed, but only for a few stanzas as she switched to another melody, blending so seamlessly that Lane almost missed the key change. He caught it just in time so he could make his own adjustment, then they were off again, the audience cheering, then clapping along.

This was by far the longest chase, or song, Ava had led him on. And the audience was loving it.

When Ava struck her final chords, Lane followed with several low notes in a row, then let the twanging of the guitar strings fade into silence.

Applause erupted, thundering throughout the arena. And only then did Lane notice that everyone was on their feet.

"More, more, more!" the audience shouted.

With the comedy club, Lane and Ava had agreed not to do encores because they didn't want to take away from the comedy acts. But now, Ava was still sitting at the piano bench, smiling at him.

"You want to do one more, babe?" he said into the microphone.

She laughed.

"I think that's a yes?" He looked out at the audience, his heart zooming all the way into his throat as everyone cheered.

"I wanted to ask a certain question of Ava before we do a second number," Lane said. "This one is personal."

Remarkably, the arena grew silent.

She fully turned toward him now, her brows lifted. "What are you doing?" she mouthed.

And then the words tumbled out. With no grace.

"Marry me."

Ava just stared at him, then her brows furrowed. "Lane . . ."

No one could hear her without the mic, only Lane could.

"We don't have to marry anytime soon," he said, the mic carrying his words throughout the whole arena. "You're still finishing school, and I probably need to work on some things, you know, to be husband material."

She was blinking rapidly. Was she crying? Did that mean she was angry? Sad?

"A year engagement is fine," Lane suggested. "Or longer?" She still wasn't answering, and his stomach twisted hard. "Whatever you decide is fine with me. I just don't want to be your boyfriend anymore. I love you too much for that."

She wiped at her cheeks. She *was* crying.

"You can say no," Lane said, although his voice felt choked, and his chest hurt something fierce. "I can handle it."

"I don't want to say no," she whispered.

Lane sure hoped he was hearing right. But she was looking at him, and her smile had appeared.

"Is that a yes, then?" he asked, stepping away from the microphone.

She nodded, then she moved off the bench and was in his arms so fast that he nearly lost his balance. He squeezed her tight. "Did you really say *yes*?" he asked against her ear.

"I did," she breathed, and then they were kissing.

Lane didn't know who started it, but he didn't want to end it. Finally, with the audience yelling and cheering, he said into the microphone, "She said *yes*, by the way."

Laughter followed.

Ava tugged him back, her cheeks pink, her eyes glimmering. "December."

"What?" It was hard to hear over the cheering arena. Why was she talking about December?

"I want to get married this December, in Prosper. Is that okay with you?"

He couldn't think of anything better. "Tomorrow or December. Whatever works."

She laughed, and then they kissed and hugged again. "We need to finish our performance, then we can figure out the rest."

"Right."

She extracted herself from his arms to sit at the piano. She played the opening stanzas of his favorite piece, the one she'd played at the competition she'd lost. But this version was altered from the original.

"I guess we're doing the second number, folks," Lane said into the microphone. He wasn't sure if his heart could expand any bigger than it was right now.

Ava grinned over at him, continuing to play, and Lane joined in. She could lead anytime, as far as he was concerned. He'd always follow. He might have some answering to do to his family, but he was one hundred percent sure that no one would be complaining. December couldn't come fast enough.

Sneak Peek!
Want to know more about Holt and Macie?
Read the first chapter of *One Summer Day* now:

Chapter 1

"Two-thousand is all I'm asking."

Holt Prosper shook his head even though his brother Knox couldn't see him on the other end of the phone call. "That's what you said last month," Holt said. "If I lend you another two-thousand dollars, you'll be in deep four thousand."

"But they put me on Granger," Knox said. "You know that bull throws everyone. The rodeo judging was rigged in Montana."

Holt couldn't hold back his scoff. His brother always had one sorry excuse after another. He'd chased his dream of becoming a big rodeo star, but that dream hadn't gone so well. He had yet to qualify for the pro circuit. Somehow, Knox had weaseled his inheritance from their dad, blown through it, gotten the girl, even married her, and now they had a kid together.

And now, Holt was standing in the living room of his family home, keeping everything together, being the go-to person in the family as usual. "I don't know, Knox," he said. The late-night call from his brother should have been warning enough. "Mom and Dad would be furious if they found out, and I don't think I can keep four thousand under the radar."

1

Holt had stayed back in Texas—Prosperity Ranch to be exact—and managed the ranch for their dad. His younger siblings were off to college, following their own ambitions. Holt wasn't one to complain. He loved the ranch. But he hated being everybody's fall-back guy. Especially Knox's.

"I'm sending half of it to Macie," Knox said, "if that makes you feel better."

At the mention of Macie's name, Holt physically reacted. He should be over it by now. The gut-punch, the racing thoughts, the slow-burn of his pulse. Macie was . . . His gaze involuntarily strayed to the family picture taken at Knox and Macie's wedding. Four years ago.

Holt rubbed his forehead, which did nothing to dispel his growing headache. "Are you ever going to tell me why you divorced her? And don't tell me what you told Mom."

Knox laughed.

Sometimes Holt hated his brother. It was complicated. The Macie staring back at him right now was how he remembered her from their first meeting when she'd come to the town of Prosper that was named after his great-grandfather and attended the hometown rodeo. Holt had even talked to her first. She'd been sweet, curious. Beautiful. Full of questions and smiles. He'd been about to ask her to the dance that followed the rodeo when Knox's name was called as the next bull rider.

Holt had told Macie that Knox was his brother, and the old saying *the rest was history* turned out to be a real thing. It wasn't the first time Knox had attracted a girl Holt had been interested in. But it was the first time Holt had cared.

"First of all," Knox drawled in a tone he usually saved for the ladies, "*I* didn't divorce Macie. *She* divorced *me.*"

Holt tore his gaze from Macie's photo, which was mocking him with her dark brown eyes and stunning smile.

He pushed out a breath. "And why's that? I thought you were her dream cowboy."

Another laugh from Knox sent heat pricking the back of Holt's neck.

"Tell you what, bro," Knox said with amusement. "Why don't you ask her for yourself? She'll be there tomorrow."

Holt stilled. It felt as if someone was dragging hot needles along his skin. "What are you talking about?"

"Didn't Mom tell you?"

If there was one thing about Knox that drove Holt the *most* crazy it was his inability to answer a question directly. Right now, though, it was imperative that Holt get his shock under control. He couldn't let his brother know how his thoughts had strayed to Macie more than once, both during her marriage to Knox, and well, now.

"Mom's been preoccupied," Holt said. With cancer treatments. And now Macie's visit might put a strain on his mom's health. She always went all-out for guests at the ranch.

Knox's next words were contrite. "Yeah, I know. Mom said she'd pick up Macie and Ruby at the airport. But, you know, if she's not feeling well, I was thinking . . ."

Another pet peeve of Holt's about his brother. Knox never asked things directly. He was a super-human-passive-aggressive type. If there was such a thing. "I'll pick them up." His tone might have come out casual, nonchalant even, but inside, all kinds of thoughts and emotions were brewing.

On second thought, maybe his dad could do the airport run.

"Thanks, man," Knox replied. "About the two-thousand. I really need it by tomorrow, or Friday at the very latest."

Holt closed his eyes. Exhaled. He had his own savings account that was separate from the ranch funds. He'd been slowly renovating a house in town. Every penny counted. "All right."

He could hear the grin in his brother's reply.

"Thanks, Holt," Knox said. "I'll make good on it, I swear."

Holt only grunted and hung up. His twisting gut told him there was little chance of Knox paying back the original two-thousand, let alone this new loan.

He slipped the phone into the back pocket of his well-worn jeans. Then he scrubbed a hand through his hair, which had been confined beneath a cowboy hat most of the day. "Macie," he said, testing the word out on his tongue.

The last time he'd seen his sister-in-law—now ex-sister-in-law—had been when she'd been pregnant with Ruby. It had been Christmas time, and Knox brought his wife home for the holidays. Macie had spent more time in the bathroom than anywhere else in the house.

Then on Christmas Eve, Knox and their dad had gotten into another argument—about money, it was always about money—and Knox had packed up his and Macie's things. And that was that.

"So . . . Macie," Holt murmured to the picture. "Looks like I'm going to be moving back to my place sooner than I thought."

No matter how much time had passed, or how much he or Macie had changed, Holt Prosper knew one thing. He'd have to return to his partially-finished house sooner than he thought. He couldn't be sleeping in the same house as her.

* * *

Grab your copy of One Summer Day wherever books are sold.

Heather B. Moore is a USA Today bestselling author of more than ninety publications. Heather writes primarily historical and #herstory fiction about the humanity and heroism of the everyday person. Publishing in a breadth of genres, Heather dives into the hearts and souls of her characters, meshing her love of research with her love of storytelling.

Her historicals and thrillers are written under pen name H.B. Moore. She writes women's fiction, romance and inspirational non-fiction under Heather B. Moore, and . . . speculative fiction under Jane Redd. This can all be confusing, so her kids just call her Mom. Heather attended Cairo American College in Egypt and the Anglican School of Jerusalem in Israel. Despite failing her high school AP English exam, Heather persevered and earned a Bachelor of Science degree from Brigham Young University in something other than English.

Please join Heather's email list at: HBMoore.com/contact/
Website: HBMoore.com

Twitter: @heatherbmoore
Instagram: @authorhbmoore
Facebook: Fans of Heather B. Moore

And yes, the Blog still lives: MyWritersLair.blogspot.com

Literary honors: 2020 Goodreads Choice Award Semi-Finalist, Foreword 2020 INDIES Finalist, ALA Best New Books - September 2020, 6-time Best of State Recipient for Best in Literary Arts, 2019 Maggie Award Winner, 4-time Whitney Award Winner, and 2-time Golden Quill Award Winner.

Heather is represented by Dystel, Goderich, and Bourret.

www.ingramcontent.com/pod-product-compliance
Lightning Source LLC
LaVergne TN
LVHW021817060526
838201LV00058B/3421